"I live my life my way and I don't make apologies for it."

"And I admire that," he murmured as his gaze locked on the tip of her tongue sliding across her bottom lip. "But you and me? Hell, you're starting something here that has nothing to do with that camp of yours."

"I hope so," Chloe said and moved in close enough that he could see down the gap of the towel to the swell of her breasts.

Then she pulled her hand free of his and laid both palms flat against his chest. She slid them up to his shoulders, to the back of his neck.

"You want to talk about the camp," she asked, "or..."

Liam looked down into those golden eyes, saw the soft curve of her smile and knew his personal fight was over. He hadn't stood a chance against this since the moment he'd walked into her office.

"What camp?" he ground out and grabbed hold of her.

* * *

Wild Ride Rancher by *USA TODAY* bestselling author Maureen Child is part of the Texas Cattleman's Club: Houston series.

Dear Reader,

The Texas Cattleman's Club has a new branch in Houston! It's very exciting for the writers because we can see old friends and at the same time, explore new territory. In *Wild Ride Rancher*, you'll meet Liam Morrow and Chloe Hemsworth.

Liam is the foreman for the Perry ranch, but he's worked his whole life to build his own fortune and chart his own future. Now he owns a ranch he's eager to get to. But first, he has to take a meeting with Chloe.

Chloe's never been encouraged to follow her dreams. In fact, she's been expected to live her life as her parents have—worrying about what everyone else thinks. Chloe's had enough. She has a plan for a cowgirl camp for young girls, but she needs Liam to convince his boss that it's a good idea.

But unexpected fireworks between them throw everything into turmoil. Liam doesn't trust the high-society girl to keep her word and Chloe has to fight to get past his trust issues. And the heat between them keeps things sizzling.

I hope you enjoy *Wild Ride Rancher*, because I had a great time writing it! Please stop by Facebook to visit and let me know what you think.

Until next time, happy reading!

Maureen Child

MAUREEN CHILD

——

WILD RIDE RANCHER

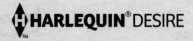
HARLEQUIN® DESIRE

Special thanks and acknowledgment are given to Maureen Child for her contribution to the Texas Cattleman's Club: Houston miniseries.

To Kelly and Julie and Anna and Jan and Verna...all good neighbors who pretend to be happy when I bring them bags of fruit every summer!

ISBN-13: 978-1-335-60356-2

Wild Ride Rancher

Copyright © 2019 by Harlequin Books S.A.

Recycling programs for this product may not exist in your area.

Printed in U.S.A.

HARLEQUIN®
www.Harlequin.com

Maureen Child writes for the Harlequin Desire line and can't imagine a better job. A seven-time finalist for a prestigious Romance Writers of America RITA® Award, Maureen is the author of more than one hundred romance novels. Her books regularly appear on bestseller lists and have won several awards, including a Prism Award, a National Readers' Choice Award, a Colorado Romance Writers Award of Excellence and a Golden Quill Award. She is a native Californian but has recently moved to the mountains of Utah.

Books by Maureen Child

Harlequin Desire

The Baby Inheritance
Maid Under the Mistletoe
The Tycoon's Secret Child
A Texas-Sized Secret
Little Secrets: His Unexpected Heir
Rich Rancher's Redemption
Billionaire's Bargain
Tempt Me in Vegas
Bombshell for the Boss

Texas Cattleman's Club: Houston

Wild Ride Rancher

Visit her Author Profile page at Harlequin.com, or maureenchild.com, for more titles.

Don't miss a single book in the
Texas Cattleman's Club: Houston series!

Hot Texas Nights
by *USA TODAY* bestselling author
Janice Maynard

Wild Ride Rancher
by *USA TODAY* bestselling author
Maureen Child

That Night in Texas
by Joss Wood

Rancher in Her Bed
by *USA TODAY* bestselling author
Joanne Rock

Married in Name Only
by *USA TODAY* bestselling author
Jules Bennett

Off Limits Lovers
by Reese Ryan

Texas-Sized Scandal
by *USA TODAY* bestselling author
Katherine Garbera

Tangled with a Texan
by *USA TODAY* bestselling author
Yvonne Lindsay

Hot Holiday Rancher
by *USA TODAY* bestselling author
Catherine Mann

One

Liam Morrow had better things to do than sit in on a meeting with some spoiled rich girl just because she'd found a new *cause*. But there was no way out and he knew it.

Irritation roared into life inside him, and Liam did his best to tamp it down. It did no good to get riled up at something he couldn't change. No matter what, Liam believed in doing his duty. He'd been raised to believe that a man's word meant everything. And he'd given his word to Sterling Perry a long time ago.

"This is what happens when you owe somebody," he muttered.

At least that old debt was nearly paid. In a month Liam would be free and clear and running his own place rather than being foreman on one of the biggest ranches in Texas.

"What was that?"

Liam looked at the man walking alongside him. Mike Hagen was new to Texas—hell, new to the Perry Ranch. But he was catching on quick, and that was a good thing, since he was set to become the new foreman here when Liam left at the end of the month.

Mike was no-nonsense and all about the job. He had ranching in his blood, just like Liam, which was probably why the two of them had hit it off right from the start. The only real difference between them was that Mike was a family man, with a wife and a baby on the way, and Liam was alone. By choice.

"It's nothing," Liam said. "Just grumbling to myself." He glanced up at the cloud-studded sky. "It's that meeting in the city I told you about."

"Ahh." Mike nodded sagely.

"Yeah, I hate getting pulled away from the ranch. Especially when we're busy. Hell, I've been trying to get out of this particular meeting for a couple of weeks."

Mike snorted a laugh. "Of course you hate going to the city. Why else would we be working with horses and cattle rather than people?"

"Good point." It was going to make it easier for him to leave the Perry Ranch knowing he was leaving the responsibility for it into good hands. Mike would take care of the land, the animals and the men who kept it all going. Sterling Perry, the owner, liked being called a rancher, but he did it from behind a desk, trusting his employees to do the actual work.

Not so different from a lot of the big ranchers in Texas, Liam told himself. In fact, the bigger the spread the less likely it was for the owner to be involved. Whether they had loved ranching when they first got into it or not, most of the owners were seduced away from the day-to-day workings by their own success, drawn into board meetings and investments and God knew what else. But that wasn't how Liam was going to run his own place.

He'd waited too long for a ranch of his own. And just a year ago, he'd finally achieved that dream. It was almost time to start living it.

Now, Liam took a deep breath and scanned the familiar yard, the outbuildings, the barns and stables. It would be hard leaving. Even strange at first. The fact was, he was proud of this ranch and all he'd done here. But it was time to move on and claim his own dreams—so he was grateful that he liked and trusted Mike Hagen. It would make it easier to walk away.

While they walked across the yard, he saw Mike lean down to pick up a hamburger wrapper tumbling along the ground, driven by the sparking wind. Mike crumpled it in one fist and looked around as if he could identify the cowboy who'd let his trash get away from him. Liam nodded to himself in approval. If the man cared about the little stuff, he'd be on top of the big stuff, as well.

"You never did say—what made you decide to leave Montana for Texas?" Liam asked.

Mike shrugged and stuffed the wadded-up paper into his jeans pocket to throw away later. "My wife's family is here and she was pining for them. With her pregnant and all, she wanted to be closer to her mother. So, being offered the job on a ranch like this one made the move easy."

"It is a fine place," Liam agreed, letting his gaze once again sweep the yard, the stables and the big main house that made up the Perry Ranch.

It was a damn showplace, but in his mind, Liam saw his own ranch. For the last year, he'd been doing two jobs—his responsibilities here and then putting his heart and soul into the future he was creating for himself. He had the land, he'd hired men and a fore-man. He'd started stocking the ranch with cattle and the horses that would be the bedrock of his place.

All Liam had to do was hold on for one more month—even if that meant taking meetings with spoiled rich girls like Chloe Hemsworth. Sterling Perry had insisted Liam meet with the woman, and just remembering that conversation from a week ago could still put Liam's back up. He replayed it in his head.

"I need you to talk to this woman," Sterling had told him that day, tapping his fingertips against his desktop. "She's been calling here nearly every damn day, and I'm tired of getting her messages. I finally told her that I was leaving the decision up to you."

Not a surprise, Liam had thought then. He'd been tossed under the bus before by a boss who only wanted the money the ranch brought him, not the satisfaction of running it.

Striving for patience, Liam had kept a tight grip on the brim of his hat and said, "I'm your foreman, Sterling. I handle the ranch, not meetings with socialites."

Sterling's eyes had narrowed on him. "As my foreman, you handle what I say you handle. And until next month, you still work for me."

Exasperated, Liam had huffed out a breath and slapped his cowboy hat against his right thigh. Frustration had swept through him, but he'd fought it down. One more month and he'd be his own damn man and call his own shots. "Fine. How do you want it handled?"

Instantly, Sterling had relaxed and an affable expression settled on his features. It was deceptive, of course. Sterling Perry was many things but affable wasn't one of them. He was stubborn and ruthless in business, but he had a way of keeping his opponents off guard until it was too late for them to get the best of him. Sterling had amassed a fortune through diversification. To him, this ranch was nothing more than a place to live and lord it all over everyone else. Sterling was, as they said in Texas, all hat no cattle.

"Take the meeting, hear her out," Sterling had said. "If her idea doesn't seem workable, tell her no. Seems crazy to me, but I wouldn't be running it. Mike Hagen would be in charge once you're gone."

"Well, hell," Liam had argued. "Have Mike meet with her."

"He hasn't been here long enough to know what would work and what wouldn't," Sterling had pointed out and narrowed his gaze on him. "And you know it." He'd picked up a pen and a sheaf of papers, effectively dismissing Liam. Then he'd glanced up again. "I've told her the final call is yours. You're the one who knows the ranch best."

A real rancher would have been embarrassed to admit that he didn't know his own ranch as well as his foreman. Not Perry.

One more month, Liam had told himself that day. After that, whatever happened at the Perry Ranch wouldn't matter to him. But even as he'd thought it, he'd known that wasn't entirely true.

His own father had once been foreman here, and Liam had practically grown up on this ranch. It would always mean something to him even though it would no longer be his main focus. So he still would look out for the ranch's long-term interests. Even while planning for his own.

"Fine. I'll meet her in Houston," Liam had said

as he'd watched his boss. "I'll give her a half hour. No more."

Sterling had shrugged. "Works for me." Then he'd busied himself with paperwork, and Liam took the not so subtle hint.

He'd stalked out of the big man's office and closed the door behind him. Meeting Chloe Hemsworth wasn't high on his list of things to do since here at the ranch they had two mares ready to foal and the vet coming to start inoculations on the cattle, not to mention the fact that Liam was busy training his own replacement. "How the hell am I supposed to work in a meeting with some society woman with too much time on her hands?"

"She's not like that."

Liam had stopped and turned toward the grand staircase that curved in an elegant sweep up to the second floor of the mansion. Esme Sterling had stood at the bottom of those stairs, and she smiled as she walked toward him.

Esme was tall, with long, straight blond hair, blue eyes that never missed much and an easy smile. In Liam's experience, she was the one exception to the rule that rich, high-society females were useless. And she was a friend.

"Didn't see you there," Liam had said, grateful he hadn't been complaining about her father out loud.

"Yes, I know." She'd shrugged, tucked her hands into the pockets of her pale gray slacks and said,

"I found out a long time ago that you can learn all kinds of interesting things if people don't realize you're around."

Liam had grinned. "Sneaky, are you?"

"I prefer covert," Esme had said, still smiling. "Look, Liam, I know my father can be…challenging."

He snorted. As a PR executive at Perry Holdings, Esme spent most of her time explaining her father's actions and guarding the family company. But of all the Perry kids, Esme had always been a friend.

"But he's right in this. I know you don't want to talk to Chloe, but she's not what you think she is."

Not convinced, he'd snorted again. "You mean she's not the daughter of a rich man with more money than sense?"

"I didn't say that," Esme had allowed. "But Chloe's more than that. She's working hard to make a life for herself, and I would think you more than anyone could understand that."

He could and that bothered him. Still, in his experience, wealthy women were mostly concerned with their hair and being seen at all the right parties.

"She's really nice and very driven," Esme had said, then paused. "Like you."

"Driven?" Liam had been unconvinced. He and Esme had been friends for a long time, so he didn't take offense at the word. But he also didn't believe it applied to him.

"Oh, please." She'd waved one hand as if wiping away his disbelief. "You've always known exactly what you want, and you've devoted yourself to getting it."

All right, he'd silently conceded, maybe driven was the right word to describe him. Liam had planned out his life a long time ago, and finally that plan was becoming a reality. "Okay, I'll give you that. But how are Chloe and I in any way alike?"

"Because she's plotting her own course, too. She's a friend, Liam, and all she's asking is to be heard."

"About a camp for little girls. On the ranch."

One eyebrow had lifted. "So only little boys are allowed to dream of being a cowboy?"

Neatly boxed in, he'd bowed his head. "You got me. I'll hear her out."

"And give her a fair chance," Esme had said.

"And give her a fair chance."

"Thanks, that's all I'm asking." Esme had walked closer. She'd reached up, kissed his cheek and patted his shoulder at the same time. "Now, don't pout because you gave in. It's so unattractive."

He'd laughed and left the house, shaking his head at the Perry family. Sterling got his way through intimidation. Esme did the same thing with a smile and reason. He preferred Esme's way.

"Hey, man!" Mike elbowed him and instantly Liam came up out of his thoughts like a drowning man breaching the water's surface. Memories of those conversations with Sterling and Esme washed away, and he faced the foreman-to-be.

"What?"

Mike laughed shortly. "You were somewhere else."

"Yeah, too much on my mind," he admitted, and couldn't wait for the day when all he had to think about was his own ranch, his own life, his own damn future.

Until then, Liam would meet the Hemsworth woman, hear her out and then get back to the real world of ranching.

Liam and Mike walked across the ranch yard toward the corral where one of the men was putting a steel-gray stallion through its paces. The horse was stubborn as hell, didn't like a bridle and pretty much thought running in circles in a corral was a waste of time. Liam couldn't blame him. It was exactly how he felt about the last several years.

Mike, already comfortable in his new role as "almost foreman," climbed the corral fence to lend the cowboy a hand. Liam watched the show, but his mind wasn't on the horse or the men in front of him. Instead, he thought about his own place, and how damned eager he was to be there.

Liam threw a long glance over his shoulder at the big house that Sterling had inherited from his late wife. Sterling Perry might not be much of a rancher himself, but the man had always loved this place and he knew how to put on a show. The house was big enough for four families to live in. It gleamed such a bright white when the sun hit it, a man could be blinded. Not to mention the hot Texas sun glancing off the million or so windows on the place. It was showy and fancy and suited Sterling down to the ground.

On Liam's own place though, the house he'd had built was a two-story log house with wide porches that wrapped around both the upper and lower floors. It was big enough for the family he might decide one day to have, but not so damn big a kid could get lost in it.

A flicker of shame slapped him as he told himself he shouldn't be thinking badly of Sterling Perry. The man had his problems, but he'd given Liam a chance when he'd needed it. For that, he'd always owe the older man.

A distant rumble caught his ear, and Liam turned his head to the southwest. Thunderheads were gathering on the horizon, big and black and threatening. As if proving itself to him, the coming storm sent a gust of wind to slap at him. The scent of rain was on that wind, and everything inside him told Liam they were in for a hell of a storm. No surprise, he thought, the weathermen hadn't forecasted it at all.

Shaking his head, he called out, "Hey, Mike!"

His replacement turned toward him. "Yeah?"

"I'm heading into Houston for that meeting. Going

to try to beat that storm back home. If I don't, you make sure the yearlings are locked down, you hear?"

He waved. "Don't worry about it, Liam. I've got it."

Nodding, Liam briefly lifted one hand and then headed for his black truck. Mike had already proved to him that he knew what he was doing, and that he'd be a good foreman once Liam's time here was done. And if Mike needed help in the short time Liam would be gone, then the other cowboys could step in.

Soon, he told himself, this ranch wouldn't be his problem. Soon, he'd be working at his own spread instead of simply checking in with his own foreman every couple days. He steered the truck down the oh so familiar drive and wondered how many thousands of times he'd driven this route over the years. Then he figured it didn't matter. He hit the Bluetooth speed dial, listened to the ring and when the foreman at his own ranch answered, Liam started talking. "Joe, you get everything tied down over there? Looks like a beast of a storm headed in."

"Just saw that, boss."

Liam smiled to himself. If there was one thing you could count on with a man who worked the land, it was that he always kept a sharp eye on the skies. Hell, weather was the one thing a rancher—or a farmer—couldn't control. So when there was a potential enemy always ready to rain down misery on you, well, that kept a man permanently on his guard.

"The boys are bringing in the mares now," Joe said. "Looks like we've got some time yet. Heck, storm might pass us altogether. But if it doesn't, we'll have everything set before it hits. Don't worry."

"I'm not," Liam lied. It wasn't that he didn't trust his foreman or the other men working for him, it was only that he'd feel a hell of a lot better if he was there, taking care of things himself.

He'd worked most of his life toward getting a ranch of his own where he would call the shots. He'd made sharp investments years ago, patented a couple of ideas he and his friends had come up with while he was at MIT and now had enough money to do what his heart had always demanded.

Funny how that had worked out. Liam's father had been the Perry ranch foreman for years, and when he died, Sterling had offered to put Liam through college with the understanding that once he graduated, Liam would come back to the ranch and work off the debt as foreman. With no other options, since his father had left more debts than money, Liam had gratefully accepted the deal.

And it was that college education and what it had enabled him to do that was allowing Liam to finally strike out on his own. He'd come out of MIT with a degree in genetics, and enough money to do what he wanted. Now he was set to undertake the breeding program he'd always dreamed of. By the time he was finished, people would be clamoring to buy mares from his herd.

There were four prize mares in foal on his ranch right now, the beginnings of that remuda he'd been working toward, and he sure as hell didn't want some storm coming in and wiping it all away before he had a shot to enjoy it. "I'll come by once the storm blows over," he told Joe.

He hung up and noticed the wild oaks lining the Perry Ranch drive were beginning to do a dip and sway in the rising wind. Scowling some, he cursed Chloe Hemsworth for dragging him away from what was important for a meeting about some camp.

Liam had never met Chloe, but he knew her type of woman. Money. Pedigree. Always moving from some charity dinner to a luncheon at the "right" place with the "right" people. She'd run with high society until she'd up and decided to open a business in Houston. According to Sterling, Chloe was running her own event planning business out of the city now.

"Figures," he muttered, steering his truck onto the road that would take him into the city. "The woman's been doing nothing but partying most of her life. Who better to throw the damn things?"

He didn't know much about her. Only that she'd been calling the Perry Ranch almost daily for weeks to pitch her idea for a cowgirl camp.

Liam had no problem with women as working ranch hands. Hell, he had a couple women working for him at the Perry place. What he didn't like was the idea of a bunch of young kids running around a ranch where they would disrupt the workdays and, worse yet, get hurt. But Sterling had ordered him to take the meeting with Chloe and hear her out. If Liam approved her ideas, Sterling would go along with it.

"Just another good reason to stop being anybody's foreman," he muttered.

His tires whined along the asphalt, and in his rearview mirror, those clouds looked darker and bigger. "This is going to be the shortest damn meeting on record."

By the time he hit Houston, Liam was on edge. The hairs at the back of his neck were standing up as the air felt electrified by the coming storm. Or maybe, he told himself, it was just this meeting that was riding him.

He didn't much care for rich, useless women trying to carve out a name for themselves. This Chloe had probably never worked a real job in her life, and was no doubt setting up shop in some fancy office where she could pretend to be the boss while she ordered a bunch of minions around. Hell, Sterling should have taken the meeting himself.

He steered around slower traffic, mumbling to himself. "Just get in, hear her out, say no and get back to the ranch. That's all you have to do."

And it was more than enough. Liam was no

stranger to rich women. Hell, before he'd had money of his own, he'd come across quite a few. In Texas, you couldn't take a step without stumbling across an oil or cattle princess. He'd even hooked up with one for a while when he was in college. Liam had believed she was different. Had thought there was a future for them somewhere down the line. Until he'd had the rug pulled out from under him. After that knock on the head and heart, Liam had learned his lesson. Wealthy, self-involved females were like Christmas ornaments. Shiny, but empty inside.

He drove into the downtown, cursing every roll of the wheel. Cities were all right for some people, but give him the empty roads of the country any day.

"Too many damn people," he muttered, and spotted the building that would be the new Houston home of the Texas Cattleman's Club.

They were spreading out from the original site in Royal, and there was already a driving fight for leadership of the new club. As a wealthy ranch owner himself, he'd be joining as soon as the club was up and running, but Liam wasn't interested in being in charge of the thing. Let the old lions of Texas fight over the club like it was fresh meat.

"Nice place, though." Even if it was in the city. He'd been to the TCC in Royal, and it was a low-slung building filled with history.

This new TCC was once a three-story boutique hotel now being rehabbed by Perry Construction.

Liam had a key to the place, since as Sterling Perry's foreman he often had to come into the city with instructions for the construction crew.

When it was finished, it'd be impressive. The third floor was bedrooms for the club president and the chairman of the board. The second floor was going to be conference rooms and offices for the TCC officers. There was still a lot of work to do on the place, but Liam knew that at least one of the suites on the top floor was finished, because Sterling had insisted on having a place for either him or other board members to stay if they had to. Sterling's insistence on his and his friends' comfort was no surprise.

Still, he turned his head from the club to the old, brick office building across the street. Liam checked the GPS just to make sure, but yeah. That was Chloe Hemsworth's address. Surprised, Liam studied the building. It had a lot of years on it, but looked sturdy enough. It wasn't what he'd pictured. He'd imagined a rich girl would want some plush, sleek, penthouse office in a modern building.

But wherever the hell she was, he had to take this meeting. Frowning, he climbed out of his truck, and tugged his hat brim down low over his eyes. The wind was still kicking, and the sudden gusts were enough to snatch a man's hat and send it to Albuquerque. Stepping around the people hurrying along the sidewalk, Liam headed for the office where the words *It's a Party* were scrawled across a wide front window in bright pink paint. Shaking his head, he opened the glass door, stepped inside and stopped dead.

This he hadn't been prepared for.

A woman—Chloe?—was bent over, picking something up off the floor. His gaze locked on that luscious curve of behind, showcased in a short, black skirt. She glanced at him over her shoulder, sent him a bright smile and said, "Hi! Can I help you?"

Slowly, she straightened up and the view only got better. She wore a dark blue, off the shoulder blouse, and her long, light brown hair lay in loose waves that kissed those bare shoulders. She wore sky-high black heels, and her gorgeous legs were tanned. Her amber eyes were wide, her mouth still curved in a welcoming smile, and all Liam could feel was the heat swamping his body.

He'd seen pictures of her of course. Like every other wealthy woman, Chloe's face was in the society sections of the Houston newspapers, and splashed all across the news website he checked every day. But she was even more gorgeous in person. Every inch of him felt tight and hot, and when she talked, he realized he hadn't heard a word.

"Sorry. What?"

She stared at him, and Liam saw a flicker of the heat that still had his body at a slow burn.

"I'm Chloe Hemsworth," she said just a little breathlessly.

That voice conjured up all sorts of interesting images in his mind, and his body responded to them instantly. She was exactly the kind of woman he avoided—and he wanted her. Bad.

Liam knew he was in deep trouble.

Two

"What happened?"

I couldn't believe it had gone so wrong so quickly.
Pacing this stupid room wasn't helping, but I felt like
a caged lion or something. Nothing I could do to
change anything and besides, if you thought about
it, it really wasn't my fault at all.

The Texas Cattleman's Club was visible from here
and I couldn't keep staring at it. The rain started
and I couldn't stop thinking about what happened.
He was all alone in there. Did he still care? Should
I have cared? No. I should have left. But I didn't.

This all started years ago, and what happened
today was just a part of it all. So really, they set it

*all in motion way back when. Today was just another
link in a long, ugly chain.*

*I did what I had to. Now, I wanted my stomach to
stop spinning and my brain to stop racing. Nothing
could change it, and I'm not sure I would change it
even if I could. I came this far, there was no going
back, and really...didn't they have it coming after
all I'd suffered?*

*Was it fair that only I was affected by those de-
cisions made so long ago? Was it fair that I'd been
forgotten and my pain buried? None of this was my
fault.*

None of it.

The cowboy was tall and broad shouldered, and
had sun-streaked brown hair that lay just over his
collar. His blue eyes were as clear as a Texas lake,
and filled with the same mystery of what lay beneath
the surface. He was staring at her with a steady fas-
cination that kindled awareness and something more
inside her.

He wore the Texas cowboy uniform of faded
jeans, scuffed brown boots and a long-sleeved white
shirt, rolled back to the elbows, displaying deeply
tanned, strong forearms. He had a tight grip on his
dust-colored Stetson, and just standing there, he
seemed to take up all the room in her small office.

Breathing was harder than it should have been,
and Chloe made a deliberate effort to drag air into

her lungs. Instant attraction roared to life inside her, but Chloe dialed it down. He was probably there to arrange a party for his girlfriend. Or wife. Still, there was something about him that was almost over-whelming. She had been born and raised in Texas, so she was no stranger to the "western man." But this one had such a compelling aura it was hard to be unaffected.

Silently, sternly, she told herself to dial it down.

"You're Chloe, right?" His gaze swept her up and down before settling on her eyes. "I'm Liam Mor-row. Sterling Perry sent me."

Stunned, Chloe stared at him for only a moment longer. She'd been expecting some gruff, older guy, with a comfortable belly. She'd never considered that the foreman of a ranch the size of the Perry place could be so young and...hot.

"Oh, well, hi. Thanks for coming," she said, rec-ognizing that she was starting to burble. She took a breath. Okay, he wasn't there to book a party, but that didn't mean he was single. "You want some coffee? Water? That's about it on the refreshment front, I'm afraid. But there's a diner just down the street. We could go there and—"

He held up one hand and, as if she'd been trained, she closed her mouth and stopped talking. Well, that was irritating.

"I'm not here for snacks," he said. "Sterling wants me to hear you out. So if you want to tell me your ideas, show me your plans, we can get through this meeting and I can get back to the ranch."

Okay, *hot* didn't excuse rude. "Wow," she said. "Thank you for your complete attention."

His beautiful blue eyes rolled. "Fine. Sorry. I'm here to listen, and that's what I'm going to do. When we're finished, I'll let Sterling know if I think it'll work on the ranch or not."

"Okay." Chloe could tell from his body language and his expression that he'd already made up his mind to say no. So it would be up to her to convince him. Well, it wouldn't be the first time Chloe had had to fight for what she wanted.

She walked to her desk, one she'd taken from her old room at her parents' house, and picked up a file folder. "Sterling actually told me that the decision would be yours because you know the ranch so well. I'm just hoping you'll actually give me a chance and not dismiss the idea out of hand."

He sighed, set his hat, crown down, on a tabletop, then folded his arms across his chest. He stood, feet braced apart as if ready for a fight and the move was so inherently sexy, she felt a fire kindle deep inside. Why she was reacting like this, Chloe had no idea. Maybe she just hadn't been dating enough. Maybe this out of the blue wild attraction signaled that she should be getting out more and spending less time on her business.

But her burgeoning company was really all she

was interested in these days. Chloe had worked really hard for a long time to break away from her parents' expectations and plans for *her* life. She'd had other dreams that had dissolved under their scrutiny, but she was fighting for this one.

"I gave my word to hear you out. That's why I'm here."

The expression on his face told Chloe that he meant what he said, and that was good enough for her. He looked resigned, but she'd take it. If he was fair, then he would realize what a good idea she was proposing. And with his support, Sterling Perry would agree to give her the land she needed on his ranch to make this particular dream come true.

"That's great." She waved him to a chair, and he looked at it skeptically. It was a delicate, cane-backed chair with a small seat and narrow, hand-turned legs.

"Maybe I'll stand," he mused.

"The chairs are stronger than they look," she assured him. Then, as if to prove it, she said, "When I was a kid, my friends and I used to stand on them to get out onto the roof so we could climb down the oak outside the house."

Both eyebrows went up. Admiration? Disbelief? Who could tell?

"Yeah," he said, shaking his head, "what were you, twelve? It's not going to hold me, so I'll stand."

She shrugged, because really, what else could she do? Once her business started bringing in steady cash, she'd buy more furniture. Right now, that wasn't high on her list of priorities. "Your choice. Now, what I wanted to talk to you about was—"

"A little girls' camp set up on the Perry Ranch."

Chloe stopped, tipped her head to one side and studied him briefly. "So Sterling told you about it."

"Enough to know it's a bad idea," he said.

Chloe took a deep breath and bit back her first, instinctive response. She'd hoped that he would come into this with an open mind, but that hope was now crushed. Arguing with the man wouldn't get her what she wanted. What she had to do was show him her plans and convince him that he was wrong. So she smiled, though it cost her.

"Not exactly prepared to give me a fair hearing, are you?"

He frowned. "I'm here. I'm listening. Convince me."

His features were closed, his eyes shuttered, but he had a point. He was there, and she had this chance to show him what she could do. Chloe was used to having to fight for what she wanted, so today was no different. If she could stand up to her father and go against all of his many plans for *her* life, then she could certainly handle this.

"Okay, why don't I show you my ideas, and then we can talk about it."

He gave her a brief, almost regal, nod. "That's why I'm here."

But would he really listen? She'd have to take her chances and be damned convincing.

"Okay, that's great." She feigned bright confidence, then motioned for him to come around her desk. Once there, she opened up the file on her computer.

She got a quick thrill when she saw the title, the name of her soon-to-be-camp, *Girls Can Do Anything*. The man behind her snorted.

Chloe sent him a quick, hard look. Gorgeous or not, she didn't like the attitude. "Do you disagree with my website design or the theme?"

If anything, his frown deepened. "I just think it's crazy to have to tell a kid they can do anything."

"Really? Even today, girls aren't given the kind of opportunity that boys are."

He snorted. "Please."

Irritated, she snapped, "Are girls told they can be ranch hands? Raise and breed horses? Herd cattle?"

With a patient sigh, he asked, "Well…they're not told they can't, are they?"

"Some are," she countered, remembering how her father had shattered her own dream of working a ranch, breeding horses. "And can I just say, you're not exactly displaying to me how objective you're going to be."

He shrugged, but she could see she'd hit her target.

"Sorry." He didn't look sorry, but okay.

"Thank you."

"Okay, show me what you've got."

Chloe took a deep breath and probably shouldn't have because he smelled really good. Not to mention that standing this close to him was making her body hum and her blood burn. Plus he was so tall. And broad shouldered. And— *Keep your mind on business*, she warned herself silently. But it wasn't her mind that was veering out of orbit.

It was her body responding to the man, and there was no way to stop it. Chloe had never experienced anything like this. Attraction? Sure. Lust? Of course. But this bone-deep burning was something new, and she was finding it hard to breathe without shattering—or worse yet, climaxing—just thinking about him touching her. Oh, boy.

"Problem?" he asked, and his voice sounded like a whisper in the darkness.

She swallowed hard. *Seriously, Chloe?* "Nope. No problem." She looked up at him and wondered if he'd moved even closer to her. How was she supposed to concentrate?

"Are you doing that on purpose?"

A knowing gleam shone briefly in his eyes. "Doing what?"

"Looming."

"I don't loom. I stand."

"Really closely."

"Worried?"

"No."

"Then no problem, right?"

"Right." All she had to do was get a grip on whatever was happening to her body. Nodding, Chloe turned back to the computer. "As you can see, I made up this website—it's not live yet, but I wanted to be able to show you exactly what I have in mind and—"

"*You* did the website?"

She looked at him and clearly saw the surprise in his eyes. "Yes, why?"

Frowning, he shook his head. "Nothing."

She knew exactly what he was thinking. How could Chloe Hemsworth have done something so complicated? Something that required talent, skills. This was not new. She was used to being dismissed. Her whole life had been spent convincing people that she was more than they thought her to be. Apparently, as gorgeous as he was, Liam Morrow was no different from anyone else she'd ever known.

"Oh, it's okay," Chloe said. "I'm used to being underestimated."

"What?"

"You know how people are," she said, looking him directly in the eye. "They take one look at me and think, *useless daughter of a rich man.* They never actually stop to think that maybe when I went to college I *learned* things. That I *earned* my degree in business."

Something flickered in his eyes, and she was pretty sure it was respect. Well, good. Chloe had dreams and aspirations well beyond the next charity luncheon. But why should anyone else believe in her when her own father didn't? And why did she care what Liam Morrow thought of her anyway? A question she couldn't answer.

"I've come across the same kind of thing," he said, and his voice was a low rumble that rattled along her nerve endings.

"Really?" Chloe smiled and shook her head. "People think you're just pretty and empty-headed?"

He grinned briefly, and that quick twist of his mouth sent a flash of heat zipping through her. Oh, probably not good. But in her own defense, she didn't think *any* woman would be immune to this man.

"No," he said with a laugh. "But most people take one look at me and see a simple cowboy."

She thought about that for a second as she stared up into his cool, blue eyes. "Nothing about you is simple, is it?"

One corner of his mouth lifted. "I wouldn't say so."

"Well, same here," Chloe told him, squaring her shoulders. "People don't underestimate me for long."

He gave her a slow, up and down look of approval and finally nodded. "I bet they don't."

Why that acknowledgment touched her, Chloe couldn't have said. She'd known him about ten seconds, right? Why should she care what he thought of her? What he saw when he looked at her? Why did she feel like her entire body was on a slow simmer?

Oh, she didn't want to think about any of that at the moment.

"Okay," she said briskly, once again turning back to the computer screen. "Back to my point. The idea is to introduce young girls—I'm thinking maybe eight to sixteen years old—to ranch life."

He frowned. "Eight's really young."

"Not too young to dream," she countered quickly. She had been eight when she'd first planned a future working on a ranch. "Every little girl I've ever known has dreamed of owning a horse. There's a connection there that should be nurtured."

"A ranch can be a dangerous place," he warned, and the frown etched into the space between his eyebrows deepened.

"I know that, I do," she insisted. "You can't grow up in Texas and not know that ranch life isn't easy. But accidents can happen anywhere. You can step off a curb in Houston and get run down by a bus."

"True, but you don't often stroll into a *herd* of buses."

"Well, I promise I won't let any of the girls take a walk in the middle of a herd. The fact that it might be dangerous doesn't mean you shouldn't go for what you want," she insisted. "As for the kids, there would be adults to supervise.

"I'm planning to have camp 'counselors' for lack

of a better word. College kids maybe." She paused, then went on faster, her words tumbling over each other in a fight to be said before she lost his attention. "Anyway, I was thinking we could have a few horses—of your choice—that are gentle with kids and we can show the girls how to ride. How to care for the animals and clean up after them. Taking care of animals teaches us empathy and patience and—"

"I get it," he said, nodding.

"Okay, well, the girls can do ranch work during the days and have cookouts and campfires at night." She clicked to the next page on her website. "This can give them the satisfaction of working, completing a task, and the opportunity to build friendships with people they might not have met otherwise. They'll learn how to do new things, get along with others and to appreciate everything they can accomplish."

"Uh-huh." He looked at the pictures of the Perry Ranch as if he were imagining a herd of girls running wild. He didn't look happy, so Chloe started talking again. Fast.

"Like I said, there would be plenty of supervision of course—"

Liam cut her off. "And some of that supervision would have to be done by the ranch hands who already have plenty of work to do." He shot her a wry look as if challenging her to dispute that.

Chloe took a breath and blew it out. Couldn't he see what she was trying to do? Of course it wasn't easy. Or simple. But how many great things were? "All right, yes, you're right. We would need some help from the ranch hands. But surely there are a few guys there who could trade off showing the girls what ranch life is like without sending the whole outfit into bankruptcy."

Outside, the wind was kicking up and spatters of rain began to pelt the windows, like dozens of fingers tapping, tapping, demanding to be let in. Inside, the room darkened, and Chloe leaned over to turn the desk lamp on.

Both of his eyebrows lifted at the sarcasm. "There's a lot of liability involved here, too."

"I realize that." And now, her own temper was beginning to spike, and it threatened to burn as hot as her blood. He was deliberately trying to squash her before she'd even had a chance to convince him. "But parents would sign legal release documents before the camp, and the ranch would be completely covered."

"I don't know about that." He shook his head, and folded his arms across his really impressive chest. If it hadn't been a sure sign that he was closing down, shutting her out, she might have allowed herself an inner sigh of appreciation. "In my experience, you bring lawyers into anything, and it all goes to hell in a flash."

Chloe sensed she was losing, and she couldn't let that happen. The Perry ranch was the best place for her to try her experiment. Mostly because Sterling had been willing to let her use his land. Most ranchers weren't open to anything that might interfere with the business. But also because she knew that ranch well, and there were a couple of female ranch hands working there too. If everything worked out there, she could start raising money to buy her own land. Of course, she'd come into her inheritance from her grandmother in five years when she turned thirty—but she didn't want to wait. She'd already waited long enough.

"This isn't about lawyers or liability," she said, meeting his gaze and silently daring him to argue. "That could all be handled. It's logistics. This is about the fact that you are simply determined to not like the idea."

"I'm determined to see the reality while you're looking at it all like a child's fantasy."

Hard to disagree, since he'd hit on the very reason she'd come up with this idea in the first place. All of her life, Chloe had been told what she *couldn't* do. And she wasn't standing for it anymore. Not from her family. Not from the hottest cowboy she'd ever seen.

"That's because it *was* my fantasy as a child," she admitted, staring at the images on the computer screen, letting herself imagine what might have been. "When I was ten years old, my father bought a ranch outside Galveston. He drove us all out there to look around, get a feel for the place." She turned her face up to his. "I fell in love instantly. The foreman showed me the horses, let me feed them, then helped me ride for the first time in my life." Her voice dropped, became a little dreamy, but there was nothing she could do about that. "I wanted to be a cowboy so badly. I had visions of growing up on that ranch, of having my own horse, of helping the cowboys…"

Silence followed when her voice trailed off until he quietly asked, "I'm guessing that didn't work out for you?"

She laughed shortly and shook her head. "No. We went back home, and my father hired a construction crew to renovate the house. I was still dreaming, planning my room, naming my imaginary horse. Then he told us that once the renovations were done, he was selling the ranch at a 'tidy profit.'"

She could still remember the disappointment, the crushing letdown she'd felt when she had learned that her father had never intended to move his family to that beautiful ranch. She'd felt betrayed, as if he'd allowed her to dream just to crush her.

"A few months later, he did sell it," she said. "I never went back to the ranch."

"So," he said, "you're trying to redo your own childhood? Is that it?"

"No," she said softly. She wasn't that foolish. But she was rewriting her adulthood far away from the plans of her father. "It's just important to me to foster other little girls' dreams. I want them to know that they can be and do anything. I know the Perry Ranch has several women working the herds—seeing that in reality would go a long way to showing the girls that anything's possible. Why is it wrong for me to want to show young girls that their dreams can come true?"

"It's that important to you."

It wasn't a question, but she answered it anyway. "Yes. It is." Her dreams had been systematically flattened by her father, who instead wanted her to marry well, have children and run the various charities he approved of. Not that she didn't someday want a husband and kids—but on *her* terms. And no matter what happened here with Liam Morrow, she was never going to surrender control of her life to anyone else.

Chloe took another breath and confessed, "This would be a test case, sort of. If it took off here, the idea could spread to other ranches, heck, other *states*."

"Big plans," he mused.

"You bet," she agreed, flashing him a quick look and a smile. "At some point, I want to buy land myself. Set up a permanent camp. Buy horses, cattle, hire wranglers, and have a place where girls can go to dream."

She watched him take her measure and saw that

he wasn't amused by her dreams, her plans. That was a step in the right direction.

"I can see how important this is to you," he said. "But I'm not convinced yet." He shifted his focus from her to the computer screen, then scrolled down the images she had posted.

"I haven't finished my pitch yet," she reminded him. And he hadn't walked out yet, either. Good sign? "If you'll check the map I posted, you'll see where I want to set up the tents."

"Tents," he repeated. "And with all these girls there, what were you thinking of using for bathroom facilities?"

Chloe winced. This was one of the sticking points she was still working out. "I thought they could use the bunkhouse—"

"I don't think the ranch hands living there would go for that."

"It wouldn't be easy, true." Actually, she hated the idea of the girls using the bunkhouse bathroom. Because it would be awkward along with a host of other possible problems. "But if that doesn't work, then maybe Sterling would let them use the bathroom off the kitchen."

"Know about that, do you?" His gaze shifted to hers.

She smiled. "I've been to the Perry Ranch many times."

"Yeah. For parties."

"You say that like an insult."

"I don't have a lot of time for parties."

"Well, maybe you should make time," Chloe countered. "It might help you lighten up a little."

"I don't do light."

She sighed. Seriously, the man was sex on a stick, but his personality was so prickly, she wondered if anyone ever got close enough to find out if he was as good in bed as she thought he was.

"All right then," she offered. "We could bring in Porta Potties for the week."

He snorted. "And portable showers?"

"These are just tiny details that I can figure out later," she said, exasperation setting in. "You're being deliberately confrontational. I wonder why."

He unfolded his arms and tucked his hands into the back pockets of his faded jeans. "Because it's my job to look out for the ranch."

"It's not like a handful of girls would be there to destroy anything."

One eyebrow winged up. "Just the working routine for the ranch hands."

"Briefly," she reminded him. "I'm thinking camp would be a week long. And I'm sure we could work out the bathroom issue," she insisted, and made a mental note to talk to the housekeeper at the Perry Ranch. Chloe was pretty sure the woman would allow a few girls to use her shower for a week.

"Look, this would be a test case. To see if there are enough girls interested."

"And if there aren't?"

"Then I drop it," Chloe said, then added quickly, "but there will be. If Sterling goes along with this, we could hold one camp week a month. I could even pay to have a bunkhouse with bathrooms built on the land." Inwardly she winced at the idea of taking money out of her savings to do it, but it would be worthwhile.

"So when you eventually move your camp somewhere else—"

Chloe shrugged. "Sterling will have a new bunkhouse he didn't have to build."

Outside, the world darkened and the wide front window rattled with a gust of wind. The rain against the glass was heavier now, a continuous assault, and pedestrians hurried along the sidewalk, looking for cover.

Liam straightened up, looked down at her and Chloe felt a rush of heat. Amazing that a man who irritated her so much could cause such a reaction.

"You said at some point you'll be looking for a permanent place?"

"Well," she said, amazed that he would ask, "yes. This isn't a one-off thing. I've been thinking about this for a long time, and I really believe that girls will love it."

"Uh-huh," he answered wryly. "And you think

Sterling will be willing to just donate you a piece of his ranch to have children running loose?"

Truthfully, she didn't know if he would or not. That would be lovely, but she had plans if that didn't happen. "I can buy land from him or maybe even another rancher not far from Houston."

He snorted.

She was really getting tired of that sound.

"Of course you can."

Chloe frowned. "What's that supposed to mean?"

"Nothing," he said. "Ranchers don't often *sell* their land. They're more interested in adding acreage to their spread. But, then again, women like you are used to getting exactly what they want from men."

"Women like me?" Irritation rose up and quickly bristled into temper. Okay, yes, she was wildly attracted to the man, but she wasn't going to stand there and be insulted. "What exactly does that mean?"

"Hey, hey, rein in your temper. No offense meant," he said, holding up one hand for peace. "I only meant that nothing comes that easy to most people. But a pretty woman can persuade a man to do most anything."

"Wow." She simply stared at him. "You're not a cowboy. You're a Neanderthal."

"Might be, but I notice you're not disagreeing," he pointed out.

It would have been hard to, as much as Chloe wanted to let him have it. Hadn't she seen it for herself most of her life? Heck, her own mother could still play Chloe's father like a finely tuned piano. And in the social circles Chloe knew best, girls were practically trained how to do the same. Pretty women turned on the charm, and that usually worked long enough for them to get their way.

"All right, there may be *some* truth to what you said…"

He nodded.

"*But*," she added, "pretty doesn't last. I use my brain, Liam. I work for what I want, and I don't use my looks or my name to take me where I want to go."

He studied her for a long couple of seconds. "I can see that. So sorry. Again. Look, I'm not a caveman and I'm not stupid. What you're trying to do is pretty tough, but if you can convince me that you can run this camp without interfering with the work on the ranch, then I'll take it to Sterling." He stopped, looked at her. "After that, it's up to you and Sterling what you work out between you. But I will say I don't see him selling you a piece of his spread."

Chloe took a breath and let it out again. She hadn't expected him to apologize or to give her respect. She just wished she knew if he meant it or if he was just trying to placate her. Either way, arguing with Sterling's representative wasn't going to get her anywhere, and the bottom line was, what he thought of her didn't matter in the slightest. She'd been alternately dismissed, overlooked and had assumptions made about her for years. Those who stood outside a wealthy family and thought it was all cotton candy and carnivals were invariably wrong, but it was nearly impossible to convince them of that.

Chloe's life had been easy as far as money went. But a soul could starve even if the body was well fed.

Yet she gave him a bright smile anyway and saw a flicker of something dart across those amazing blue eyes. It was there and gone again so quickly, she couldn't be sure exactly what it was, but her body reacted anyway. Honestly, it was getting harder to keep her mind on the business at hand—in spite of the irritation he could spike in an instant. Still, she tried.

"Okay, like I said before, what I want to do is introduce the girls to ranch life," she said, warming to her theme the second she started talking. "Most of them will be from the city and completely unaware of a world where there isn't traffic and noise and so many lights you can't see the stars at night."

He gave her a thoughtful look. "Sounds like you're speaking from experience."

"I grew up in Houston, and the only time I got to see the stars was when I visited my grandfather in El Paso."

"Is that what fixated you on ranch life?"

"It is," she said as memories flooded her mind. Smiling to herself, she admitted, "Once my father sold my 'dream ranch,' I spent lots of time with my grandfather. I'm sure I got in the way plenty, but I helped the men working for my grandfather when-ever I was there. They taught me how to care for a horse, how to ride and that hard work was the only kind of success that mattered."

His eyebrows lifted. "Your father was okay with that?"

"No, not really," she admitted. "But my mom was. She'd grown up on that ranch, and wanted me to have the same experiences. Mom died when I was four-teen, so the visits to the ranch ended. My grandfa-ther died a couple of years later, and my father sold that ranch too."

Nodding, he asked, "So you're doing all of this as a way of spitting in your dad's eye?"

Surprised, she had to admit, "No. Well, in a way, that's true, I guess. Hadn't really thought about it, but yes. I'm a disappointment to him, I suppose, but my younger sister, Ellen, is exactly the type of daughter he wanted us both to be."

One corner of his mouth lifted briefly, and Chloe felt a quick rush of heat.

"And what kind of daughter is that?"

"Malleable," she said with the slightest twinge of sorrow. "I love my sister, but she's more willing to let our father direct her life than I am. And wow, that sounded terrible, didn't it?" Guilt roared into life in-side her. "We're not very close and I regret that, but I just don't…get her, I guess."

And *why* was she making this confession to a man she didn't even know?

"I can understand that," he said. "I don't really get you, either."

Chloe laughed. "Okay, that's honest. I like honest. But seriously, what's not to get?" She'd been completely forthright, and actually even more truthful than she'd determined to be. Why for heaven's sake had she told him about her parents and her sister and her grandfather? That had nothing to do with this meeting. "I don't know why, but for some reason I'm telling you things I had no intention of telling, so you probably know me better by now than my sister does."

"All right," he conceded with a nod, "maybe it's not that I don't get you—but more that you're not what I expected."

"You mean I'm not talking about manicures and my last trip to Paris?"

He shrugged, and that action made his chest shift and move in a really enticing way. *Keep your mind on the camp, Chloe.*

So she gave him a bright smile. "Well, then, I'm going to take that as a compliment."

"You really should," he told her and his blue eyes flashed again, threatening her concentration abilities. "So show me more."

Three

Clinging to hope, Chloe went through her sample pages, one at a time. The Perry Ranch was well-known in this corner of Texas, and had been photographed hundreds of times. All she'd had to do was use some of those photos that had been in countless magazines and have her friend Curtis Photoshop girls into the images.

Outside, the day got darker, the rain hammered the window like tiny fists demanding entry, and the rising wind rushed down the street with gleeful abandon.

But for the next half hour, Chloe didn't notice. She gave her spiel on how great the ranch camp would be for girls, and Liam listened. He paid attention. He asked great questions and even made a suggestion or two. She assured him that she would be there herself to keep the girls out of the working cowboys' way. In fact, Chloe was starting to feel more than hopeful. One corner of her mind began to plot and plan, sure that he would come down on her side. That he would talk to Sterling and her dream camp would become a reality. If he said no now, she'd be crushed. "I've really thought it all out. It's been building in my head for years."

"I can see that," he said, nodding.

"And not only would this be great for the girls, but it's a publicity treasure for the Perry Ranch," she added, dangling that thought like a worm on a hook. "Think of the goodwill Sterling would get for hosting and funding this ranch camp."

He was still nodding, so Chloe took that as a good sign.

"Really, the funding would be just a drop in the bucket to Sterling Perry, and he would be the talk of Texas."

"He'd enjoy that," Liam murmured.

She grinned. "The funding would be mostly on covering food and the tents where the girls would stay. I'd want the camp itself to be free to underprivileged kids and maybe a modest cost to those who could afford it."

"I'd want the camp to start this June." She could see he was doing some fast thinking. Yes, it was already April, but she didn't want to lose another summer. If she started in June, it wouldn't be much, but it would be a beginning. "We'd probably just have a handful of girls for the first camp, but by July we could handle a dozen or more."

"And you'd be there? Overseeing it all?"

"I would." She winced internally at the thought of being away from her new business for days at a time, but she had a cell phone; she could work through email and her tablet had a good battery. She could do this. She *would* do this, if it meant success.

"I'll think about it," he finally said.

"Really think about it," she asked, "or pretend to think about it while giving it a few days before calling to say no?"

One eyebrow lifted. "When I tell you something, it's the straight truth. I said I'll think about it and let you know. And I will."

"Okay, I believe you. But don't make me wait too long, all right? I'm not really patient, and the wait will probably kill me."

He laughed shortly. "Gotta say it again, you're nothing like I expected. So I don't know what to make of you yet."

"And that's important?"

"Good to know who you're dealing with."

"Fair point." After all, she didn't know quite what to make of him, either. She knew she wanted him. Knew he could be irritating. But beyond that he was a mystery, and maybe that was feeding her body's reaction to him. "If you say yes, we'll get to know each other really well, because I'll be at the Perry Ranch until the end of the month."

He frowned and she had to take that as a bad sign. "Yeah," he said thoughtfully, "you would be."

Into the suddenly strained silence, he turned his head to stare out the window and into the street beyond.

"What is it?"

"Take a look at that. The storm," he murmured, narrowing his gaze on the rain, now coming in sideways, riding the wind. The downpour was so heavy, it was as if it were erasing the world it rained down on. "Saw it on the horizon when I left the ranch. Thought we'd have a few hours. We don't."

"That looks bad," Chloe whispered. And even as the words slipped out, she recognized them as a major understatement. Lightning cracked the sky, and thunder rolled down with a deafening *boom*. When a heavy storm like this roared into Houston so quickly, it meant flooding wasn't far behind. She'd seen it before and the currents that swept away cars, animals, even people.

"We should go." Liam grabbed her arm, but Chloe pulled free long enough to snatch up her purse and tuck her tablet inside. Slinging the bag over her shoulder, she hurried behind Liam as he strode for the front door. They hadn't taken three steps when a sudden microburst of wind hit the big window, shattering it. Liam whirled around, pulled her in tight against him and tucked her head down against his chest.

Liam felt the power of the wind and the slash of the rain, but neither of them, luckily, had been cut by the glass. The back of his shirt and his jeans were soaking wet, but he didn't feel any pain. They'd gotten lucky. Chloe had her arms wrapped around him and he felt her shaking. Easing back just far enough that he could look down into her eyes, he shouted, "You okay?"

Stupid question, but she nodded, looking past him at the devastation of her office. The wind howled like damned souls released from Hell, and the heavy rain swept into the room like a blanket of water. Everything was wet and glass was everywhere. Outside, the streets were already flooded up to the curb and the water was still rising. With so much water coming in so quickly, the city's drains couldn't keep up. The flooding, he knew, would get worse.

"Are you all right?" She had to shout to be heard over the wind.

He kept one arm around her, snatched up his hat from where the wind had blown it, then pulled it down tight on his head. "Yeah. Fine. We've gotta get clear of this."

"My car's down the street."

His sharp laugh was cut off abruptly. "No way in hell are you driving in this. My truck wouldn't make it so a car never will."

He pulled her up close to his side and ignored the flash of burn he felt with her body pressed so closely to his. He'd been fighting the draw toward her since the moment he'd walked into that office, and it wasn't getting easier. They had to get to safety. The question was…to where? Liam knew that in a few minutes his truck would probably be floating down the street, so they had to find somewhere close to hole up.

Then he looked out the broken window and saw it. "We're going over there."

She swiped wind-driven rain off her face, and pushed her sodden hair back from her forehead. "The new Texas Cattleman's Club?" she asked. "It's not open. It's not even finished."

Lightning lit up the sky again and was reflected in her pale brown eyes. Over the crash of thunder and the screaming wind, Liam shouted, "I've got a key. Even if the first floor floods, one of the rooms on the top floor is mostly finished. We can wait it out there."

She looked around as if trying to find another option. He could have told her there weren't any. They were stuck together. The city was shut down but for emergency vehicles by now, and it'd stay that way until the storm blew through.

Finally, she nodded.

"Good enough." He gave her a nod and a tight smile. "I'm going to hold on to you. That water in the street is rising fast, and the current's like a high-running river. Just grab hold of my belt and don't let go." He kept one arm wrapped around her, his hand settling just beneath her left boob. Ridiculous to be noticing in this situation just how good it was to have his hands on her. "You ready?"

Chloe nodded. Snaking one arm around his waist, she grabbed hold of his belt and ducked her head against the rain when he led her out of the office.

Icy cold water sloshed against their shoes, their ankles and all too quickly, their shins. The water was rising even faster than he'd thought it would. Not surprising. The rain was coming down in a thick sheet now, showing no signs of easing up. Stepping off the curb into the river that was the street, Liam fought against the current to keep his balance and to keep Chloe safe.

Overhead the sky was almost black with menacing clouds. Jagged claws of lightning briefly flashing in the darkness. The rumble of thunder was a constant roar. The sidewalks were empty, people having long ago headed for cover. If he hadn't been distracted by Chloe while she gave her pitch about a kids' camp, he might have noticed the change in the weather in time to avoid being half-drowned.

But that was done. All he could do now was keep her safe and get them both somewhere dry. "Come on," he urged, his muscular arm tightening around her, "keep moving. Don't stop—you could get swept away in the current."

The middle of the street looked like a whitewater river not a main street in downtown Houston. Parked cars were rising off the ground to bob and sway in the current like a fisherman's lure. It might take hours for the water to recede, and that would be *after* the storm stopped.

Chloe turned her face against Liam's wet shirt and everything in him tensed. Hell of a time to have his own dick distracting him. He ignored his own personal agony and concentrated on reaching safety. Every step felt like a victory as they leaned into the wind, headed inexorably for the new Texas Cattleman's Club building.

"Almost there." He lowered his head to her, and still, he knew his voice was nearly lost in the punishing weather.

"Thank God," she shouted back.

He dipped his head into the wind, pulled her up onto the sidewalk and then moved her to stand between him and the building as he dug out keys to the TCC. In a few seconds, he had the door opened, them inside and the door closed and locked behind them. But a lot of water had already rushed in, and now it was pushing up under the front door. Those few seconds with the door open had given the rain freedom to sweep inside, wetting down the whole front hall.

"Won't these windows shatter, too?" Chloe wiped wet hands across her wet face, and even with her hair plastered to her head and her eye makeup all smeared, she was still one of the most beautiful women he'd ever seen.

He shook his head and stepped back from her. "Probably. But they haven't yet, so we're in better shape than we were at your office."

"That's true." She looked around then, and Liam followed her gaze.

The first floor was covered in painter's tarps. There were sawhorses scattered about and a few tools the crew had left behind. It was a room under construction, and the only thing it had going for it at the moment was that they were out of the cold and wet and noise. Then Liam looked down to where the water was still sliding through under the door frame.

"We go up," he said, motioning toward the renovated grand staircase that sat in the middle of the room like an aging queen who'd had a makeover.

"This will flood, won't it?"

As she said it, gusty winds rattled the windowpanes, and one of them on the other side of the room broke under the force of it. Rain and wind raced through that opening, and the other windows rattled again as if preparing to shatter themselves.

"Yeah," he said. "It will. Probably soon. The construction crews started at the top and got one room done, at Sterling's orders, before they went back down to the first floor. These old windows haven't been replaced yet, and there's enough water pouring in under the door frame that in another hour, we'll be ankle deep—if it takes that long."

"Right."

Houston was such a cosmopolitan city, outsiders tended to forget that though it was sophisticated and civilized, this was still Texas and the weather could turn on you in an instant. Floods were all too common, so he knew well enough to take cover and wait it out. Liam had seen the devastation left in a flood's wake, though he'd never been caught up in one himself.

They were being pelted with rain, and the wind, as it swept through the broken window, felt icy. He grabbed her hand and tugged her behind him. "Okay, let's go."

She stepped out of her heels, and barefoot, she was just a tiny thing. A protective instinct rose up in him, and he didn't even try to stop it. Would have been pointless anyway. Halfway up the staircase, they jolted in tandem when the rest of the windows blew in. They both paused, turned to look at the damage, then Liam caught her hand in his and held on. "We go up."

He'd keep her safe. Safe from the storm, anyway. Liam groaned inwardly. Hell, she'd be safe from him, too. But he wasn't going to be comfortable anytime soon. Not with his body burning and his mind dredging up image after image of Chloe Hemsworth and him, naked, wrapped together. Gritting his teeth, he shut down his thoughts for his own good.

He had to give her points. She kept up with his much longer legs by running up the stairs beside him. They paused on the second-floor landing, and Liam looked around as if to reassure himself that all was well. Still needed paint and the new flooring was stacked against one wall. But it was warm and dry, so that was enough. Wouldn't do them any good. Then he put a hand at the small of her back and steered her up the stairs again.

Here there was a wide seating area, complete with wet bar and flat-screen TV. There were two short couches, chairs and tables boasting brass lamps with Tiffany shades and it looked, he thought, like a damn oasis after the weather they'd just escaped.

"There are two bedrooms up here," he said, walking toward a door on the right. "This one's for the TCC president and the other, when it's furnished, will be for the chairman of the board, or visiting guests."

"When it's furnished?" she repeated.

"Yeah." He knew what she was thinking because it had occurred to him, too. There was only one bed in this place so they'd have to share. Or, Liam thought, maybe he should sleep on the wood floor. Or he could curl up into the fetal position and try to sleep on the miniature couch. A little discomfort might keep his head clear.

He opened the door to the furnished bedroom and stared. Something stirred inside Liam and he tamped it down. One look at that big bed, covered in a dark red comforter, boasting a mountain of pillows against its carved oak headboard, and all he could think about was throwing Chloe down onto it and rolling around with her for a good long while. But he couldn't do that, so he told his treacherous brain to stop providing tempting images.

"The water's still rising," she said, and thankfully dragged Liam out of his thoughts. He shifted his gaze to her, standing at the window, looking down. In a few long strides, he joined her there and took in the scene below. The water was up past the wheel wells on the parked cars, and the wind was bending the trees in half. Lightning flashed in the sky and thunder rolled out around them, loud enough to carry through the double-pane windows.

"And," she said in a mutter as she looked down at the phone in her hand, "cell service is down. Perfect."

He glanced at her. "Who would we call anyway? Emergency teams have more important things to take care of, and no one could drive through this mess anyway."

He thought about the Perry Ranch, and hoped that Mike and the hands had gotten everything taken care of. Then his thoughts turned to his own place.

It was new, and the most important thing in Liam's life. But worrying wouldn't get him anywhere, so he pushed the anxiety away. He held on to the thought that he had good men working for him, and his foreman was smart and knew what to do. "We're stuck here for a while."

"How long?"

"How the hell do I know?" He snapped it, then shrugged his shoulders as if sloughing off the rotten mood. "Sorry. I don't know. But there's food here. The construction guys keep a refrigerator on the ground floor stocked." He thought about the fact that water was rushing in downstairs, too. "Why don't you go and take a shower? Warm up, get out of those wet clothes. They've got it stocked with towels and soap and all. I'll go down and raid that fridge before it's under water."

She looked up at him and her pale brown eyes looked like gold. He felt that rush of heat that had swamped him at first glance of her. When she licked her lips, his groin went hard as concrete. He'd be lucky to be able to walk in another minute.

So he tore his gaze away and looked around the room instead. It was set up for VIPs, so there was a small refrigerator at the private wet bar as well as the one in the main room. He hoped it was stocked because he could sure as hell use a beer.

"I'll be back," he said tightly, and headed for the door. At the threshold, her voice stopped him.

"Thanks."

He looked back at her. "For what?"

She shrugged, a simple motion of her shoulders and yet, her dripping wet shirt tightened across her breasts, feeding fires that wouldn't go out.

"For being there, I guess," she admitted. "If I were alone when the storm hit, I probably would have tried to drive out of the city."

"You wouldn't have gotten far."

"I know," she said wryly. "That's why 'thanks.'"

"You're welcome." She was glad he'd been there. He was wishing he'd been anywhere else. Because now, he was trapped in a luxuriously appointed bedroom with a soaking wet woman with pale brown eyes. Shaking his head, he muttered, "Go take that shower."

Then he left.

On the other side of the city, the floodwaters were higher and still rising. Ryder Currin grabbed a fifty-pound sack of flour from the homeless shelter's pantry and slapped it down in front of the door to keep the water from sliding in.

"This is a darn shame, Mr. Currin," the shelter manager said. "You just brought us these supplies."

Ryder turned his head and looked up at the older woman. "Not a problem, Mavis. I'll replace anything that gets ruined. But this sack of flour should help keep us dry—for a while, anyway."

He looked around and saw that several of the men had nailed plywood sheets across the windows. Good thing the shelter had their tornado supplies in the back room, too. This way the windows wouldn't break. Of course, it was dark as a cave now, so all the lights were burning and Mavis and her assistant had gathered up old-fashioned hurricane lamps in case the power went out. Which it would. Just a matter of when.

He'd only stopped by today to drop off a load of provisions, but the storm slamming down onto the city with no warning at all had trapped him here. Along with a handful of workers, a few of the people who regularly looked to this shelter for help, and… Angela Perry.

It must have been the Universe having a laugh at his expense to put the one woman he didn't want to see in a room where he couldn't avoid her. She didn't look any happier to be trapped alongside him, and he couldn't really blame her for that. Hell, he could still feel the slap across the face she'd given him at the TCC fund-raiser last month.

He was eleven years older than Angela, and she was the daughter of Sterling Perry, Ryder's enemy. But still, he couldn't help looking her way whenever her back was turned.

"Will you need that last sack of flour?" Mavis asked, bringing him back to the task at hand.

"I don't think so." He stood up, looked around at

the brightly painted walls, the family-style tables
and the long serving counter that was now crowded
with sandwiches, a kettle of fragrant soup and a huge
urn of coffee.

Looking back to the woman in front of him, he
said, "We should be able to ride this out. We've got
enough food and plenty of space for everyone."

She nodded. Mavis had been running the shelter
for ten years, and she didn't shake easily. A black
woman with sharp brown eyes and a no-nonsense
attitude, Mavis ran a tight ship.

"We might have more people wandering in here
for help, too, so you'll be in charge of lugging that
fifty-pound sack out of the way."

"Yes, ma'am," he said. Then while she continued
to talk, Ryder's gaze slid past her to Angela. She was
handing a sandwich and a bowl of soup to a young
man who winked at her in thanks. Ryder was captivated by her.

Somehow, Sterling Perry, a man to whom money
and position meant everything, had managed to cre-
ate a daughter who was completely at home in a shelter, helping others. She was a mystery and damned if
Ryder wasn't intrigued. It seemed Angela had more
of her late mother, Tamara, in her than her father.

Ryder had been friends with Angela's mother,
too many years ago to count. And that thought reminded him that he had no business looking at this
woman and wishing things were different. He was

too old for her. There was too much drama in the past still snaking into the present. And then there was the fact that at the moment, Angela hated his guts.

She wore a deep blue shirt, gray jeans with black boots and somehow looked elegant even under the circumstances. Her blond hair hung in a straight, golden fall to her shoulders, and her blue eyes picked up the blue of her shirt and shone even brighter than usual. He wanted to talk to her. To explain a few things, if he could.

It was only recently he'd heard the rumors that she'd no doubt been listening to just before she slapped him. Ryder wanted to tell her that he'd never had an affair with her mother, Tamara. That he hadn't blackmailed her and that her mother's father had willed Ryder that land twenty-five years ago because Ryder had been Tamara's friend when she hadn't had another.

He really wanted things set clear between them. She deserved the truth, he told himself sternly. Of course, it had nothing to do with what she made him feel whenever she was within five feet of him. And hell, even he didn't believe that. But as much as he wanted to talk to her it would have to wait because her safety and the safety of everyone at the shelter had to come first. Even as he thought it, someone pounded frantically on the door.

"Open up!"

Instantly, Ryder bent down to shift the heavy bag from in front of the door, then swung it wide. A young couple with two little kids looked like drowned rats as they squeezed through the door, chased by pelting rain and the call of thunder.

"Wow, it's ugly out there," the man said, holding out one hand. "I'm Hank Thomas. This is my wife, Rose, and our kids, Hank junior and June."

Ryder looked at the kids. The boy was about five and June closer to two. They looked tired and cold, and their mother seemed to be on the ragged edge.

"Looks like you've been out in it a while," he said.

"Truck got swamped when we tried to get out of the city," Hank told him, and swept his son up into his arms.

"We didn't know what to do," Rose added, swaying her daughter on her hip. "Then we saw lights through the cracks of the plywood on your windows."

"Well, you're welcome here. Let me get you some towels to dry those babies off," Mavis said, bustling up and taking charge.

"Thank you," Hank said, and dropped one arm around his wife's shoulders.

Ryder felt a pang of envy. He still missed his wife, Elinah, and didn't see nearly enough of his grown children. He was alone now, and he didn't much care for it.

"Go on with Mavis. She'll fix you up with soup

and coffee," he said, then smiled at the boy. "And maybe a cookie or two."

He watched them go and saw Angela look up as the family approached. Then she looked past them right into his eyes, and for a heart-stopping second he felt the hard punch of connection even from across the room. There was something between them. Something he hadn't counted on. That he'd thought had died when he'd lost his wife, Elinah. Elinah had been his miracle. He'd already had one marriage fail when he met her. She'd seen something in him worthy of taking a risk and he never stopped being grateful for that. Elinah became his second wife and the woman he had been born to love. When he lost her, Ryder had felt as if his life was over. Now he was waking up again and he wasn't sure what to do about it.

His heart heavy, he walked off to the supply room to search for some towels. Sooner or later, he would find the chance to talk to Angela. He just had no idea if it would clear things up or make everything worse.

Liam frowned at the water pouring through the first floor of the Texas Cattleman's Club. Already streams of water were washing across the floor, snaking through the rooms, claiming more and more territory. Rain raced through the broken windows, soaking him further as he stood there. Since he couldn't do anything about the damage, Liam trudged through the mess to the back room. The refrigerator was big, but not exactly full. Using a box off one of the tables, he filled it with the sandwiches, fruit, some crackers and a half a bag of chips and bottles of water he found in the fridge, then trudged back through now shin-high water to the stairs.

Back in the bedroom, he heard the shower running through the closed bathroom door, and tried not to think about a wet, naked Chloe. Instead, he stocked the bar fridge with his loot and helped himself to a beer. While he drank it, he walked to the window and looked down at the mess that was Houston.

The rain hadn't let up a bit, still pouring down in what looked like an unending deluge. Which meant the floodwaters would continue to rise, and he didn't know how long they'd be stuck together. With no phone, no way out of this sanctuary, it was as if he and Chloe were trapped on an island. Just the two of them.

"Damn it." He took another pull on the beer bottle, then set it aside to take off his sodden shirt, his boots and socks.

He was wet to the bone and still it couldn't quench the fires blistering his blood. Liam heard the shower shut off, and instantly, his mind provided him with images designed to bring him to his knees. Chloe, warm and wet, stepping out of the shower, grabbing

a towel, smoothing it up and down her body and—
"Oh, yeah. This is great."

"What?"

He'd been so caught up in his own imagination he hadn't heard her open the bathroom door. Now he turned to look at her and his mouth went dry. Her hair fell long and damp to her bare shoulders. She had a thick, sea green towel wrapped around her and knotted between her breasts. Her bare legs were honey colored, and her toes boasted a deep purple polish. Everything about her made him hunger.

"Nothing," he managed to say in spite of his suddenly dry mouth. "I, uh, found some food downstairs. Plus the wine and beer in the bar fridge. You want anything?"

"Wine would be good."

"Right." Liam was grateful for the task that would give him something to do besides stand there staring at her, fighting the urge to touch her.

"You know," she said, "as long as we're here, you could tell me what you're thinking about my plan for the camp."

He looked back over his shoulder at her. She was sitting on one of the two chairs drawn up to a gas fireplace that he should probably turn on.

"That's what you want to talk about?"

"Why not? We're stuck here, right?"

"Yeah." He carried the wine back, handed it to

her, then hit the switch for the fireplace. Instantly, flames leaped into life on artificial logs.

He took a seat opposite her. Those eyes of hers were mesmerizing, and he couldn't seem to look away. What did he think of her plan? Personally, he thought it was a good idea. Made him remember being a boy, following his father around the ranch, learning about horses, conserving water for the cattle herd and dreaming of one day having his own place. Besides that though, he had three females working for him on the Perry Ranch, and they were every bit as good as any of the men. They could ride, train, herd, do most anything asked of them. Why shouldn't girls be allowed to dream of being ranch hands?

On the other hand though, if he said yes, and made the recommendation to Sterling, then he'd have to spend the next few weeks dealing with Chloe. And Liam didn't want to have to deal with wanting and not having her on a daily basis. If that made him selfish, he'd just have to live with it.

"So?" she prodded, and Liam stood up, unable to sit still while his mind worked and his body wept.

"So, I'll think about it," he said a little hotter than he'd planned.

"What is there to think about?" she countered, standing up, too. She took a deep breath, and that knotted towel dipped in response.

He gritted his teeth. "Look, you made your pitch,

I listened, but I'm not going to be rushed into a decision."

"Who's rushing? We're talking. You could tell me what you're thinking," she demanded.

He snorted.

"I'm really tired of that sound," Chloe said, eyes narrowing.

"I'll make a note," he ground out and walked away from her toward the window. Better to keep a safe zone between them. He should just go and take a shower, but damned if he wanted to get naked around her. As it was, standing too close to her was more temptation than he could bear.

She followed him. *Of course she did.*

"Why won't you just tell me what you're thinking?"

His gaze shifted from the storm to her eyes, and he read a different sort of storm in those golden depths. And he knew she wasn't talking about the camp anymore. "Trust me, you don't want to know what I'm thinking right now."

"What if I do?" She moved in closer.

"Then you're crazy."

"That's been said before," she admitted, tipping her head to one side to stare up at him. "You are seriously the most irritating man…"

"Good," Liam told her. "Hold that thought."

"…and the most gorgeous man I've ever met."

He stifled a groan. He really didn't need the complication that could rise up from whatever was happening here, so he brushed that aside with a laugh. "Yeah, I'm a beauty."

She reached up to slide the tips of her fingers across his bare chest, and he hissed in a breath in reaction.

"Why am I so drawn to you?"

He grabbed her hand to keep her from touching him again. "Temporary insanity."

She grinned and her whole damn face lit up. Those eyes of hers were pulling him in, and Liam didn't know how much longer he could resist what she was plainly offering. His gaze dropped to the towel again, and he found himself willing that knot to loosen.

"Looks like I'm not the only one temporarily crazy."

He looked into her eyes again. "Maybe it's contagious."

"Wouldn't that be nice?" She smiled and the curve of her mouth made him want to kiss her, drown in her.

He made one more attempt at extricating them both from the situation. "Chloe, don't start up something you'll regret later."

She sighed and shook back her still-damp hair. "I don't do regrets anymore, Liam. I live my life my way, and I don't make apologies for it."

"And I admire that," he murmured as his gaze

locked on the tip of her tongue sliding across her bottom lip. "But you and me? Hell, you're starting something here that has nothing to do with that camp of yours."

"I hope so," she said, and moved in close enough that he could see down the gap of the towel to the swell of her breasts. His body clenched, and it took everything he had inside him to keep from grabbing hold of her and losing himself in her.

Then she pulled her hand free of his and laid both palms flat against his chest. She slid them up to his shoulders, to the back of his neck. At the same time, she went up on her toes and stopped when her mouth was just a breath from his.

"You want to talk about the camp," she asked, "or…"

Liam looked down into those golden eyes, saw the soft curve of her smile and knew his personal fight was over. He hadn't stood a chance against this since the moment he'd walked into her office.

"What camp?" he ground out and grabbed hold of her.

Four

This was a nightmare. When they found out, what would I do?

The storm was raging, so for right now, there were no worries. No one would discover what had been hidden. But when the storm ended...

What should I do then? God, how had it even happened? I lost control, that's all. It was an accident. I had to remember that.

Beyond the window, the world was dark, but for the flashes of lightning. Rain swept down from the sky and flooded the streets, sending cars sailing along the road like colorful boats with no rudders.

Emergency vehicles were out. Flashing red lights pierced the darkness.

And out there was the secret. Hidden now.

But for how long?

Screw complications. Liam didn't give a good damn what happened after this moment in time with her. He'd wanted her since the instant he'd seen her. Since then, she'd irritated him, intrigued him and completely captivated him. And now, she was killing him.

His mouth covered hers and her soft gasp of pleasure filled him, rushing through his body, speeding along the licks of flame dancing in his bloodstream. His tongue parted her lips and she took him in, welcoming him with an eagerness that nearly did him in. She met him stroke for stroke as their tongues twisted together, leaving them both breathless.

Her hands slid up and down his bare back, her short, neat nails dragging along his skin, setting tiny fires everywhere she touched, and Liam had to have her. Fast. He tore the towel from her body. She gasped and tipped her head back as his hands covered her breasts, his thumbs and fingers tugging at her hardened nipples. He bent his head for a quick taste, then indulged himself by sliding his big hands down to cup her bottom and squeeze. She ground her hips against his groin, nearly sending him over the edge.

Hell, he hadn't felt this randy since he'd had his first woman when he was sixteen and stupid. *Stupid*.

Warning bells went off in his mind and he pulled his head back, struggling for air. For control. Breathing hard, Chloe swallowed, licked her lips and looked up at him in stunned surprise.

"Why'd you stop?"

His chest was tight, his dick screaming and his mind was shattered, and still he managed to say, "No condoms. We can't—"

She blew out a breath, tossed her drying hair out of her eyes and asked, "Are you healthy?"

"Of course I'm healthy," he said, a little insulted. "Are you?"

"Sure am," she said, grinning. "I'm also on birth control."

"Hallelujah," he muttered and grabbed hold of her again, keeping her pressed tightly to him. Then he spun around, put her back to the wall and reached down to undo his jeans. "No time, Chloe. Just no time at all to waste."

"Agreed." She lifted her legs, hooked them around his waist and held her breath, waiting. "Do it, Liam. Now."

She didn't have to wait long. Liam freed himself and in the next instant slammed his hard length deep inside her heat. It was like coming home. That was the only clear thought in his mind, then it shut down, drowned out by his body's reaction to hers.

He kissed her, hard and long and deep. Their tongues came together again, frantically, desperately. Breath swished from one to the other and back again. Their bodies moved eagerly, hungrily, each of them chasing that elusive explosion of release. Chloe's heels dug into the small of Liam's back as she pulled him in deeper with every stroke.

He'd never had a woman like her. Never felt this incredible rush of heat and desire and satisfaction all at once. Never had a woman react like this, so wildly, so freely. He relished every gasp and sigh, the feel of her fingers clutching at his shoulders.

"Harder, Liam," she urged. "Harder."

He'd been holding back, not wanting to hurt her, but her broken plea snapped his internal restraints. Like a tiger slipping a leash, Liam charged. Again and again, he pounded away at her until both of their bodies were screaming with desperation.

Outside, the storm seethed in counterpoint to the storm raging between them. He looked into her eyes, watched them glaze over as she shrieked his name and her internal muscles clamped around him. He felt her climax as if it were his own and an instant later, he let go and emptied himself into her, riding that wave of release like a triumphant warrior.

Half-blind, breathless, he rested his forehead against hers and fought for air.

"Oh," she said on a rush of breath, "that was…"

Liam nodded. She couldn't find a word to describe

what they'd just survived, and neither could he. It was enough to know it had happened. And would happen again. And again.

"Yeah," Liam agreed. "It was." Keeping their bodies locked together because damned if he wanted to pull away yet, he turned around, walked to the bed and sat down with her on his lap.

She tossed her head, throwing her hair back, and grinned at him. "Cowboy, if you can do that against a wall, I have to wonder what you can manage on a bed."

Liam smiled back. Damned if he'd ever had a woman as sexually in tune with him as Chloe Hemsworth seemed to be. And that grin of hers was infectious. But his smile died away when she twisted her hips, grinding her body against his. He groaned tightly at the friction she created between them. His body burned anew, and in seconds he was ready to go again.

"Well, ma'am," he drawled, staring into those magic eyes of hers, "why don't we find out?"

He dropped one hand to her bottom and the other to the hot, wet center of her where their bodies were still joined. She jolted the instant his thumb stroked across that tight sensitive bud of flesh.

"Liam…" She moved on him, against him.

He stole a quick kiss and continued to use his hands to push her higher. "Damn, you feel good."

Her eyes locked on his. "You know, I really do."

He grinned. Hell, he'd never had this with a woman. The smiles, the laughs, the…connection.

He liked it. All of it. But now wasn't the time for thinking that through.

"Get out of those jeans," she ordered on a whisper.

"Right." Shifting slightly, Liam laid her down on the bed, pulled away from her and in seconds was out of his jeans and grabbing her up again.

"Oh," she said softly, stroking her hands up and down his thighs, "that's better."

"Yeah, now I want a taste." He dipped his head to take one of her nipples into his mouth.

"Oh, you can taste me as much as you like. You have a magic tongue, Liam…" Her fingers speared through his hair, holding his head to her, silently insisting that he not stop, that he take more. So he did. His lips, teeth and tongue worked that hardened, dark pink nipple until Chloe was writhing beneath him. He slid one hand down the length of her body and dipped one, then two fingers into her heat. Instantly, her hips came off the bed and rocked into his hand.

"Two can play this game," she whispered. Then she did a little torturing of her own. She reached for him, curled her hand around his hard length and stroked him lightly until his eyes were burning from the fires within. When she curled her hand around him, rubbed her finger across the tip of him, Liam nearly lost it.

"No more games." He pulled away, sat back on his haunches and drew her up and onto his lap. She went up on her knees and then slowly lowered herself onto him. Inch by agonizing inch she took him inside, and the whole while their eyes were locked, each of them watching the reactions of the other. That fire within him erupted into something wild and out of control. And he didn't bother to try to stop it. Instead, he threw himself into the flames, dragging Chloe with him.

When she'd taken him in fully, she ground her hips against him, twisting, turning. He lifted her high enough to be able to take one hard nipple into his mouth. He wanted the taste of her filling him as completely as he was filling her.

She threw her head back, arched her spine and kicked up the rhythm she'd set. Together they moved in a rush of sensation, in a frantic need to recapture that release they'd both shared only minutes ago. He had to have it. Had to have *her*. Liam didn't know how he could want so completely so quickly, but it didn't matter. All that mattered was the next touch, the next kiss, the next taste.

His hands dropped to her hips as he steered her into an even faster rhythm. They were breathless now, and staring into each other's eyes again. As if it meant life itself, neither of them spoke. Neither of them looked away. The only sounds in that room were their ragged breathing, the slap of two bodies coming together and the incessant slash of the rain against the windows. Thunder boomed out as an exclamation point when Chloe finally shouted his name, digging her fingernails into his shoulders.

He didn't stop. Kept pushing on, higher, faster. Liam wanted her to come again, this time *with* him. And as the first eruptions in her body eased, he sensed her tightening all over again.

She shook her head, breathing hard. "Liam, I can't…"

"Yeah. You can," he whispered, burying his face in the curve of her neck, inhaling her scent, taking her inside him until every breath was flavored with her. "You *will*. Come with me, Chloe. Come again."

Trembling, she clung to him, gasping as new need erupted inside her. He tasted her pulse, felt the rush of blood in her veins and the hammering of her heartbeat and knew she was close. So was he. Liam felt as if he'd explode if he didn't let go, and still he maintained control. He knew if he held on only a moment longer, he'd feel their bodies shatter together. He was only half sane now, Liam thought. His mind was closing down. And it didn't matter. Nothing mattered but the woman already screaming.

As she clutched his shoulders and helplessly rode him, Liam finally surrendered and a roar shot from his throat as his body joined hers in a tangled knot of need and release.

And in the silence following, they fell together.

They spent the night exploring each other, having a picnic of cheese, crackers and wine in bed, and finally each of them caught a couple of hours sleep near dawn. With the storm still raging, Chloe was now wrapped in a blanket in front of the fire staring at the man across from her.

A real cowboy, Liam had that look of supreme self-confidence about him, not to mention that he really was almost too gorgeous. Miles of muscled, tan flesh. Eyes that burned with passion and secrets she wished she could read. And holy hell, what he could do to her body. Chloe had never known a night like the one she'd just lived through. Never thought her body was capable of feeling so much. His passion, his tirelessness, bordered on magical.

Liam poured her another glass of wine and leaned back against the chair behind him. The lamps were burning against the storm's darkness, and the fire sent flickering shadows into the room.

Chloe sipped at her wine, then took a bite of one of the sandwiches Liam had salvaged from the downstairs refrigerator. She really couldn't believe everything that had happened since the day before. A simple meeting about the girls' camp had become so much more. All because of the storm still huddling over Houston. Her gaze slipped to the window, where rain slapped the glass and flashes from the lightning made those drops shine like diamonds.

"Doesn't look like it's letting up anytime soon," Liam said.

"We're stuck here then." Chloe looked at him.

His dark brown hair was a little too long, which only gave him a dangerous look as the shadows and light of the fire danced across his features. The blanket he sat on was draped across his groin, leaving his tanned, muscled chest bare. Chloe sighed a little, remembering the feel of all that hard, hot flesh pressed against hers.

She'd never felt anything like she had with Liam. Okay, she hadn't been with a lot of men, but she wasn't exactly a timid virgin, either. And in her experience, Liam was…she had to admit, *amazing*. Instantly, her mind went back to the hours they'd spent together. Sex had always been nice. But sex with Liam was a life-changer. He made her feel so much she hadn't been sure she could contain it all. And yet here she was, hours later, wanting more.

"Looks that way," he said, looking away from the fire to lock gazes with her. His lake-blue eyes shimmered in the firelight and seemed to burn just as hot as the flames.

"I checked cell service while you were taking another shower," he said. "Still nothing. And I'm guessing it'll only get worse. We'll lose power for sure. I'm only surprised it hasn't happened yet."

The instant he said it, the lights blinked off, and startled, Chloe half laughed. "You should use your power for good, not evil."

One corner of his mouth quirked, and that action tugged at something inside her. "I'll try to remember." He glanced at the gas fire, still burning merrily. "We've got this for light, anyway. Want more wine?"

"Sure." Wine for breakfast. This was new. But somehow, it was as if they were out of regular time, so who cared? She held her glass out and watched as he filled it with a gold liquid that shined in the glow of the fire. Then he filled his own glass and lifted it in a toast.

"Here's to…storms and surprises."

She smiled and took a sip, still staring into those mesmerizing eyes. "You surprised me, too."

"Not exactly the way most meetings end up," he acknowledged.

"Not mine, anyway," she said, taking another sip of wine. Chloe sat quietly thinking for a second or two, then asked, "Do you hate the idea of a girls' camp?"

He studied the wine in his glass for a long minute, before lifting his gaze to hers again. "Seriously? You want to talk now?"

She shrugged. "Well, we're not exactly busy, are we?"

He nodded. "Not at the moment. Okay then. No, I don't hate it. Hell, I understand it."

"Really." It wasn't a question, but she wanted an explanation anyway.

He stretched out his legs, and Chloe's gaze dipped briefly to where only a corner of the blanket now lay across his groin. She took a breath to cool the rush of heat to the pit of her stomach, but it didn't help.

"Remember, I grew up on a ranch." Then he drew one knee up and laid his forearm across it. The blanket shifted again, and Chloe forced herself to keep her gaze focused on his eyes.

"Did you always live on the Perry Ranch?"

He nodded. "Most of my life, yes. My dad was the foreman there, and he taught me everything he knew about ranching—and that was a hell of a lot."

"Now I'll be jealous," she said, shaking her head. "I grew up taking piano lessons and dance lessons that would have served me well in eighteenth-century Vienna."

He snorted a laugh, and Chloe realized she didn't mind the sound so much anymore. "At least they also gave me riding lessons, so a part of my yearning to be a cowgirl was fed at the local stables once a week."

He studied her over the rim of his wineglass, and Chloe wondered what he saw when he looked at her. "How did you come to be Sterling's foreman?" she asked. "Was it handed down from your father?"

"In a way," he said, taking another sip. "When my dad died, Sterling offered to put me through college if I came back after graduation to work off the debt." He shrugged. "Seemed like a hell of a deal to me. So I went to MIT—"

"Why MIT?" She frowned a little at the thought

of a real Texas cowboy going to school in Massachusetts. "Why not UT or Texas A&M?"

That corner of his mouth tipped up again. "I wanted to see something of the country, I guess. Spread out from these hills and oaks." Lightning flashed and thunder boomed. He waited until it was quiet again to continue. "MIT has a great genetics program, and one of the things I'm going to focus on at my ranch is breeding. I wanted to learn all I could."

"Did you?"

"Yeah, I did," he said, lifting the glass to look at the wine with the firelight shining through it. "Me and a couple of other guys came up with a few things while we were there and took out a few patents."

Her eyebrows arched. "Patents? On what?"

"A couple on different methods of breeding."

"There are different methods?" she asked, grinning.

"I suppose there are." He smiled. "For horses, anyway. Then we came up with a couple of other little things."

"You're a man of many talents, aren't you?"

"Well now," he said in a soft drawl, "you're in a better position to know that than I am."

She smiled and her body tingled. "Good point."

"Anyway," he said, "after graduation, I came back here and took the foreman's job for Sterling. In a month, I'm done, though."

A jolt of something that felt an awful lot like regret whipped through her like one of the bolts of lightning streaking across the sky. "You're leaving?"

He shook his head. "No. Just moving on. I've got my own place now, and in a month that's where I'll be."

"Your own ranch?" Her voice sounded wistful even to herself. "The envy continues."

He smiled easily. "Can't blame you. The land I picked up is beautiful. A few thousand acres of grassland and hills. It's perfect. Got the house built last year, and the first of the herds I'm going to build are already in place."

It sounded wonderful to Chloe. All of it. The fact that he'd gone away to college, proved himself and now was building the dream he'd wanted for years. She'd joked about being envious, but the truth was, that's exactly how she felt. Liam Morrow was building the life he wanted while Chloe was living a second choice dream. Yes, she enjoyed the party planning, but her heart was still in ranching. Being a part of the earth, raising horses, working with them. And that's really what had inspired her girls' camp idea. She did want them to dream and reach for those dreams, but it was also a way for her to live out what she'd been denied.

He was still talking, describing the ranch he was building, and Chloe could see it all in her mind. It sounded wonderful and she'd love to see it in person.

She wondered if this encounter with Liam would go on or if it would end with the storm.

"One thing I don't get to this day," Liam mused.

"What's that?"

"Well, all the time I've been on the Perry Ranch, I've never seen Sterling take even the smallest interest in it." Liam frowned into his wine. "He likes the house all right, likes the power of being one of the biggest ranchers in Texas, but he couldn't give one single damn about the operating of it. I guess it's that he has a love-hate sort of thing for the ranch. Just can't figure out why."

"You don't know?" Chloe gave a short laugh of surprise.

"Know what?"

The firelight danced and flickered around the darkening room. Lightning flashed in the sky and the rumble of thunder was like a constant drumbeat.

"Oh, Cowboy, you have to get off the ranch once in a while," Chloe said with a shake of her head. "How else will you keep up with the gossip?"

"Not interested in the local grapevine, thanks."

"But that's where all the information you want is," Chloe teased, and when she didn't get any reaction at all, she sighed a little and said, "Men clearly have no appreciation for the little things. Sterling Perry loves that ranch but you're right, he hates it too."

"That's not telling me anything I don't already know."

She took a sip of wine. "I'm just getting started. Sterling's still furious over his late wife, Tamara, and the red-hot ranch hand she had an affair with."

"What?"

Grinning now, Chloe got into storytelling mode. Fine. Gossiping wasn't nice, but she wasn't too proud to admit that she liked keeping up-to-date on what was happening—and didn't mind sharing with the pitifully ignorant. "Sterling was actually the foreman on what was then the York Ranch. Then he married the owner's daughter, Tamara. The rumor is that Tamara apparently had a passionate affair with one of their ranch hands. Ryder Currin."

"Currin?" Liam blinked. "The oil baron?"

"The very one," Chloe said, and held her glass out for Liam to refill it. Once he had, she leaned back against the chair behind her and settled into talking. "Tamara was ten years older than Ryder at the time, but apparently that didn't stop anything. They say the affair kept going on even when Ryder was married. It was the talk of the town back then. I know because my mother and her friends aren't exactly known for their whispering talents."

"How did I never hear any of this?" he asked.

"Clearly, you're not hanging out with the right people," Chloe told him. "Anyway, when Tamara's father died, Sterling could finally get off a horse and into an office. He fired Ryder, and no one saw him again until the will reading. Tamara's father left

Ryder a strip of land and not too long after that, Ryder struck oil."

"It sounds like a soap opera."

"Doesn't it?" she asked brightly. "Anyway, Sterling was furious about Ryder's inheritance and started talk that Ryder actually blackmailed Tamara into getting her father to leave him the land. Even though Tamara passed away years ago, Ryder and Sterling are still mortal enemies. Doesn't that sound dramatic?"

"That's one word for it. But how do you know if any of it's true?"

She lifted one shoulder and let the blanket slide down just a bit. She was rewarded when she saw his eyes flash. "Of course, there's a chance it's not true at all. But, after watching my own parents wheel and deal all my life, I'm really not surprised by any of it."

"Your father had an affair, too?"

She laughed and shook her head. "Oh, no. My father only cares about perception. How things look to the outside world. He and my mother are quite alike there. Neither of them would ever have an affair because then they might not be thought of as perfect anymore." Chloe actually winced when she'd finished, as if she couldn't believe she'd just said all of that to a virtual stranger. A stranger who knew every inch of her body. She shivered.

"Wow. You don't hold back, do you?"

She met his gaze and shook her head. "No. I grew

up on polite lies and pretension. That's not how I'm going to live my life anymore. Don't get me wrong, I love my parents—I'm just not interested in being what they want me to be."

"Which is?"

"Do you really care about all of this?" she asked suddenly. "I mean yesterday we didn't know each other at all."

"And today I know you've got a birthmark shaped like a teardrop on the inside of your right thigh," Liam said softly.

Heat pooled in her core as she remembered just how much attention he'd paid to that particular mark. And how much she wanted him to repeat that experience.

"So to answer your question, yeah. I really want to know."

Nodding, Chloe took another sip of wine. "Okay. They want me to be another link in the Hemsworth chain. Don't stand out. Don't be different. March in lockstep with family tradition and don't draw attention to yourself." She stopped, inhaled sharply and said, "Wow, that sounded really bitter, didn't it?"

"Little bit," he agreed. "But I get it. You want to run your own life. Hard to argue with that."

"Thank you," she said, "but you'd be surprised how few people I know agree with you."

He gave her a long look. "Maybe you know the wrong people."

Maybe she did at that. After all, her friends were women she'd grown up with, who were all taking the route expected of them. She was the black sheep. The one who made waves and trod down the path less traveled and good God, how many clichés could she think in one sentence?

"Well, now I know you." *Really* well, she added silently.

"Yeah," he said, "you do."

"Don't sound so excited about it."

He smiled a little and shook his head. "No, I'm just doing some thinking."

"About?"

"That camp of yours."

Chloe held her breath. Judging by his expression, he wasn't going to be giving her the answer she wanted. So even before he spoke, Chloe prepared her arguments.

"I'm willing to try it."

"What?" Stunned, she could only stare at him.

"Yeah, surprised me too," he admitted. "But I'm willing to give this a shot under one condition."

Chloe held her breath and waited.

Five

Angela Perry took another batch of corn bread out of the oven and set the tray on a wire rack to cool. Setting the hot pads aside, she walked back into the main room and saw a few new faces. The rain was still falling, though it seemed to be easing up a bit now. Still, it didn't stop stranded people from making their way into the shelter. The roads were still impassable, so she was grateful the shelter was well set up to handle a crowd.

Children shrieked with laughter and chased each other through the worried adults, huddled together in small groups. The scent of coffee hung in the air, mingled with the aroma of a huge pot of chili.

There were cots dotting the main floor and volunteers streaming in and out of the kitchen. But she had eyes for only *one* of those people pitching in to help.

Ryder Currin.

Angela hadn't seen him since that fund-raiser for the Houston TCC. The night she'd overheard the ugly rumors about Ryder's affair with her mother. The night she'd walked right up to him and slapped him across the face in front of everyone.

She closed her eyes briefly at the memory. Yes, she'd been furious. But more hurt than anything else. How could she be so attracted to a man who had *slept* with her *mother*?

"Oh, God…"

"Are you okay, honey?"

Angela took a breath and smiled at the woman looking at her through worried brown eyes. African American, Mavis was short, curvy and her gray hair was cut close to her head, the better to display huge gold hoops dangling from her ears. She kept the shelter running, donations pouring in and made sure everyone who stepped through the doors felt welcome and important.

Angela considered herself fortunate to have such a friend. "Yes, Mavis, I'm fine. Thanks. Just tired, I guess."

And she felt ashamed of herself for saying so. Mavis had been cooking all night, serving the people who staggered in wet, bedraggled, terrified and had hardly sat down for a cup of coffee.

Angela had been working with Mavis here at the shelter for a few years now, and the woman never looked tired, despite having at least twenty years on Angela. The woman was an inspiration and, apparently, indefatigable.

"Oh, you go and sit down for a bit." Mavis gave her a one-armed hug and a pat. "Have some tea. Good for the body, good for the soul."

Right now she could use both. Angela was tired, true, but that wasn't really bothering her. She'd been tired before and would be again. It was Ryder Currin haunting her. She couldn't stop looking at him. Watching him.

"I can plainly see who you've got your eye on," Mavis mused with a knowing smile.

"What? Oh." Caught, she simply stopped talking. No point in trying to deny it after all.

Smiling, Mavis said, "I saw Ryder helping you bring in the extra cots from the supply room."

He had. In fact he'd helped her several times during the storm. He'd been polite, respectful. He hadn't once brought up the TCC party or the slap—though Angela had the feeling he wanted to talk to her. She just hadn't given him the chance, because she wasn't at all sure she wanted to hear what he might say. But in spite of everything, there was a simmering burn between them she couldn't deny. Just looking at him from across the room made her heart beat a little faster, fanning the flames of a slow simmer in her blood.

"Ryder's a good man," Mavis said. "God knows, he's been a big help to us here at the shelter."

"Well, we're all doing what we can in an emergency."

"Oh no, honey." Mavis shook her head and patted Angela's forearm. "It's not just this storm. Ryder's been helping us out for years."

"Really?" Stunned, Angela stared at her friend. How could she not have known that? She'd been working with the shelter for a long time and until today, she'd never run into Ryder. She wouldn't have pictured him as a man interested in volunteering. Giving back. Was that terrible of her? In her defense, she'd never seen her own father care about anything outside the business and the family name. Heck, most men with the kind of wealth Ryder Currin had amassed were only interested in getting more.

"Oh yes. You saw that new Viking stove we've got in the kitchen? Ryder bought that for us." Mavis gave the man a smile, though he didn't see her do it. "His late wife, Elinah, God rest her, was very involved here at the shelter. And he came along most times, I think because he was just so crazy about her."

She paused and the expression on Mavis's face became reflective, sympathetic. "Since he lost her, I think this shelter represents his last link to her. He donates food, those cots you carried in, so many things. I couldn't name everything he's done for us. And he never even accepts a thank-you. A good man," she said with a wink, "and a stubborn one. He's had his troubles, we all do. But he reaches out to people, and that says a lot about him as far as I'm concerned."

It said plenty, Angela agreed silently as Mavis moved off to help a young mother with her baby. Watching Ryder now, Angela tried to compare the man she thought she knew with the one Mavis had just described. If he'd loved his wife Elinah so much that he continued with her contributions to the shelter as a tribute to her, could he really have cheated on her with Angela's mother?

Now Angela had to wonder if she'd made a mistake in believing those rumors.

As if he could feel her gaze, Ryder suddenly looked up and across the room, straight into her eyes.

Angela felt a rush of something confusing swim through her bloodstream. Drawn to him, horrified by the rumors about him and her mother and touched by what Mavis had said about the man, she felt as if she had been blindfolded and spun in circles. She simply didn't know what to think anymore.

As if hypnotized, Angela stood perfectly still and watched as he walked toward her, a tall man in a long-sleeved white shirt, black jeans and hard-worn, black boots. His dark blond hair was a little long and his dark blue eyes shone with purpose as he approached, and Angela thought she'd never seen a man walk with more confidence, more rugged masculinity oozing from every pore. And she had never in her life met a man who affected her as he did.

The question was, had her mother once felt the same?

"Angela," he said when he stopped just inches from her, "I think we should talk about what happened."

Would talking make it worse? She didn't know. "Ryder—"

He held up one hand, but it wasn't a command for quiet, more of a silent plea for her to listen. "I know why you slapped me that night." His voice was low and soft, and he gave a quick look around to be sure they weren't being overheard. Then he looked at her with such complete focus she felt as if he were staring directly into her soul. "Look, I heard the rumors you must have been reacting to. I couldn't believe they were springing up again, like mushrooms after a hard rain." He shook his head and muttered, "Probably because of the new TCC. People just naturally take sides in old rivalries."

"That's what this is? Rivalries?"

He looked at her. "Honestly, I don't know. What I do know is that it's just rumors. Angela, I'm asking you to let me tell you the truth."

His eyes met hers and held her in thrall. That's the only word that could explain why she felt as if she were caught in amber. Paralyzed. Unable to look away.

What she might have said, Angela wasn't sure, but whatever it was died unuttered when the young couple who'd arrived a few hours ago with their two small children came rushing up. The man—Hank—grabbed Ryder's arm.

"Our little girl's missing. Our Junebug. She's just..." He looked around, clearly frantic. "Gone."

Hank's wife, Rose, slapped one hand to her heart and kept a firm grip on her little boy with the other. Tears filled her eyes and spilled down her cheeks. "She was there a second ago. I turned to talk to someone and when I looked back..."

Mavis was nearby and overheard. She hurried to join them, swept that scared little boy up into her arms and said, "Now, don't you two worry. I'll take care of him. You all go find little June. She's probably scared and lost, poor thing. This old building is so big, even I get turned around from time to time."

"She's right." Ryder took charge and Angela had to admire that. His voice was low and steady, and got through Hank's panic and Rose's fears. "Mavis will take care of your boy, and you don't need to worry on that score. Hank, you and Rose take the upstairs. Angela and I will search down here." He reached out and clapped one hand on Hank's shoulder. "Don't worry. She can't have gone far. We'll find her."

"Okay." Hank took a breath and seemed to gather

himself, reaching for strength for his wife's sake, if not his own. "That's a good plan." Hank grabbed Rose's hand and the two of them headed for the stairs.

Ryder shot Angela a quick look and said, "All right, let's go." He crossed the floor with long, measured strides, headed for the main supply room, with Angela right behind him. "We'll start here, then hit the kitchen and the service porch. You'll have to look everywhere. A child that small can squeeze into unbelievably tiny spaces."

In the supply room, Angela stopped and stared. There were towers of supplies, boxes stacked everywhere and tables and cabinets and who knew how many spots that a little girl might hide herself in.

"Look," Ryder said as he strode to the back of the room to start searching, "there's never going to be a good time to do this, so while we look, I'm going to talk."

"Now?" Angela asked, opening a cupboard, looking in, then closing it and moving onto the next one.

"Yeah." He moved methodically, she noticed, checking every square inch of the crowded, yet organized room. She looked through cabinets, behind stored boxes of blankets and towels and under tables. Ryder did the same, moving quickly, but thoroughly.

While they searched, Ryder started talking and Angela was more or less forced to listen.

"Like I said, I know what you heard." He checked behind a wall of boxes, then straightened up and looked at her. "But it's not true. None of it. I was your mother's *friend* twenty-five years ago. That's all." He stared hard at her, willing her to believe him. She could see, even from across the room, that his eyes were hot and clear and determined.

"Tamara didn't have anyone else to talk to back then. I was young and she seemed lonely and—" He paused, took a breath. "Anyway, we never slept together. Never so much as kissed. As for my land that your father thinks I blackmailed Tamara's father for?"

She waited, not knowing what to think. What to feel. Angela was torn. She really wanted to believe him—not just because she was so attracted to him, but because she didn't want to think her mother had cheated on her father.

Ryder checked the last cabinet, then straightened up and faced her again. "Tamara convinced her father to will me that land as a thank-you for listening to her when she had no one else."

Her heart hurt for the woman her mother had once been, and if what he was saying was true, then Angela was glad to know Tamara had had Ryder to talk to. She was still turned around. Still confused—by this man and what she felt for him.

"I don't know what to say," Angela finally whispered.

"You don't have to say anything, not now. I had to put all of that out there, to clear the air. I don't need a response from you, Angela. I just needed you to know the truth."

Ryder headed for the door, holding out one hand toward Angela. "Right now though, we've got bigger problems. We've got to find that little girl."

She slipped her hand into his and felt a zip of heat. She knew he felt it too because she saw his eyes flare. Then he folded his fingers around hers and tugged her along behind him. Their own personal drama would have to wait.

They started in the back—they checked the service porch where the washing machine and dryer were roaring with the latest loads. They checked the back door leading to the small yard and saw it was locked with a dead bolt, so there was no way the child could have gotten out into the rain and rising waters.

They checked the walk-in pantry and a storage space. No sign of the child. Angela's nerves started screaming. "Where could she have gone?"

"Kids can disappear on you in a heartbeat," Ryder said, still searching while he talked. He felt that they were on a more even footing now that he'd told Angela the truth. Even if they hadn't talked about it, at least he'd said his piece. "I remember when my Annabel was two, Elinah had sent us to the store for something or other. Turned my back for a second and she was gone. Don't think my heart beat again until I found her, curled up and asleep under a rack of ladies dresses."

God, it didn't seem that long ago. That made him old as hell, didn't it? A man with no business looking at Angela Perry the way he did. Feeling for her the way he did. Struggling to keep his own brain on track, Ryder gave Angela another memory.

"Then there was a time you and your mom had a fight. You were a teenager, home from boarding school and got yourself into such a temper, you took off into the night. Tamara asked me to find you. Do you remember that?"

She stopped, looked up into his eyes and said, "I remember. You found me out by the stock pond. I was so mad."

He smiled. "Yeah, you always did have a temper." Then he rubbed his cheek as if her slap was fresh.

"I'm…sorry about hitting you. I shouldn't have."

He shook his head. "Don't worry about it. I'm sorry about a lot of things that we don't have time to talk about at the moment."

She nodded and maybe he was fooling himself, but Ryder thought her eyes looked clearer, less ready to spit ice or fire at him. That was good enough for now.

"Come on. We'll look in the kitchen." And that's where they found June, a few minutes later, curled up under a table, completely hidden by a tablecloth that fell to the floor.

"Oh, thank God," Angela whispered as she smiled at the sleeping child. "She looks so peaceful, while the rest of us are frantic."

Ryder scooped the child up into his arms and she snuggled in close, sighing in her sleep. He missed this, he realized. Having a child in his arms, counting on him, needing him.

"Poor baby, she must be exhausted," Angela said, leaning across him to smooth the child's hair back gently.

Ryder turned to her, their faces just inches apart. His heart gave a hard thump as he looked into her beautiful eyes. He wanted her to believe him. *Needed* her to. "There was nothing but friendship between your mother and me, Angela."

"I really want to trust you, Ryder," she admitted. "But I need some time to think about all of this."

It wasn't a perfect response but it was better than he'd expected. "That's fair," he said, and took her hand briefly in his. "I can wait."

At the touch of her hand, he felt a swell of protectiveness rise up inside him, along with something else that he really shouldn't have been feeling.

"Come on," he said abruptly, shattering whatever spell was building between them. "Let's get her back to her parents."

"Okay," Angela said and gave him a soft smile.

For now, that was enough.

Liam stared at Chloe for a couple of silent seconds, trying to talk himself out of what he was about to do. She was a society woman, he reminded himself, just like the one he'd fallen for six years before. But even as that thought settled in, he had to admit that if he'd been stranded in a flood with Tessa, she'd have complained nonstop.

He couldn't see her enjoying a picnic of cheese and crackers and warm wine on the floor in front of a gas fireplace. She'd have worried about her hair and her manicure and her makeup. She'd have had him running in six different directions trying to keep her happy. It shamed him now to remember that he had done just that for six long months. Until she'd tossed him aside for a richer, older man desperate for affection.

Chloe wasn't Tessa. She'd stood up through all of this. She hadn't complained once. She'd laughed with him, given him the best damn sex of his life, and all in all had forced him to at least adjust his opinion on rich women. Well, *this* rich woman at any rate. That didn't mean he was looking for anything permanent, though. He had a lot of work to do on his life before he even thought about having a woman or a family in it. And when it was time, he wouldn't be looking at women like Chloe.

Because as much as she intrigued him, she came from a world so different from his, she might as well be from Mars. He wouldn't be forgetting that again. For now though, for a brief hookup with no strings, Chloe Hemsworth was a man's dream woman.

But she had as much chance of running a ranching camp as he did of playing the tuba with the local symphony. She was a stubborn woman though, so Liam thought the best way to convince her that this camp wouldn't be an easy task was to show her just what ranching was like, up close and personal.

Forget the romance of the cowboy-cowgirl thing. He knew what she was thinking because her fantasies about the life had been built as a child. While Liam had grown up with the reality, Chloe thought of ranching and saw images of campfires, beautiful horses who never bit or kicked and cattle that followed her around like pet dogs.

What he had to do to end this idea was to show her what the real life was like. The sunup to sundown work. The dirt, the sweat, the bone-aching misery when you finally lay down to go to sleep. That should ease her back from this dream without him having to actually crush it himself.

"Look," he said finally, "I'm willing to give this a shot. You come out to the Perry Ranch. Stay there for the next couple of weeks. You follow me and the new foreman, Mike, around and learn what you can about ranching and how your camp would fit in with a working ranch."

"Stay?"

Yeah, he told himself it wouldn't be easy having her so close to hand day and night. But if he could get past that, then he'd never have to see her again and that would be best. He already needed her more than he was comfortable with. If he spent much more time with her, he'd only get drawn in deeper. So if she agreed, he'd put her up in his guest room, work her ass off, then send her back to the city and to the world she really belonged in.

In fact, he knew just the way to sweeten this pot enough that she wouldn't be able to say no to the idea.

"No other way to find out if this is going to work or not." He drew one knee up, and didn't even notice that the blanket covering his groin slid off. Resting his forearm on his knee, he stared at her. "You can't sit in Houston and decide to be a ranch hand. You say you've been thinking about this for years, but you don't really know what it all entails. You have to find out what you're getting into and so do we.

"If it works out, I'll give you the land for your camp on *my* ranch." Saying that cost him some, but Liam told himself she'd never make it. Soon enough she'd realize that this wasn't what she really wanted. So he wouldn't have to worry about having her permanently at his place. "You won't have to deal with Sterling or do more convincing. So that's the deal. You up for it or not?"

"You'd give me room for the camp on your land?" She sounded disbelieving, and he couldn't really blame her.

"That's what I said." He pushed one hand through his hair. "Look, even if I recommend this idea to

Sterling, he'll still want to negotiate with you. You're not ever going to have free rein on the Perry Ranch. But, if you prove yourself, you can have that on the Morrow ranch."

He watched her, and could have sworn he heard the gears in her brain turning as thoughts raced through her mind one after another. She bit her bottom lip, and Liam focused on that action. On her mouth. He wanted her again, and told himself that having her on the ranch and not *having* her wasn't going to be easy.

"My schedule's clear for the next three weeks," she mused. "The next event I'm handling isn't until next month. Mr. and Mrs. Farrel's fiftieth anniversary party."

"Congratulations," he said, shaking his head.

"And I can keep up with plans and arrangements by email." She looked at him. "You do have internet, right?"

Wryly, he said, "No, but we've got homing pigeons you can use. Of course we've got Wi-Fi."

"Right." She took a breath, and he watched her breasts rise up beneath the blanket wrapped around her. "Okay, then yes. I'll do it."

"It's not going to be easy," he warned, giving her an opportunity to back out now.

"I'm not worried."

She should be.

"Where will I stay?"

"At my cabin," he said, and saw a fire in her eyes that matched his own.

Yeah, none of this was going to be easy.

Six

Once the storm was over and the floodwaters started receding, they left their temporary nest to explore what had been left behind.

The streets were still covered in muddy water, but no more than an inch or two when they walked outside for the first time since taking refuge in the TCC.

"It's a damn mess," Liam mused, looking up and down the street.

Chloe followed his gaze, and noticed that others were streaming from offices and apartment buildings to look around. A few of the trees planted by the city were broken or had branches missing from the gusting winds. Windows were shattered and several cars were now parked on the sidewalk, covered in water and mud.

"It's going to take some time to clean all of this up."

"It will," he agreed. "But I can't hang around for that. I've got the Perry Ranch and my own to check in on."

She understood that, even though she felt a pang of regret for their time together ending. But she had plenty to do as well, before she could take up his challenge on the ranch.

"You going to be all right?" Liam watched her with a steady gaze.

"I'm fine," she assured him. "You go on. I've got my car, remember? Should be dried out enough to use. And if it's not, I'll call my dad, get a ride to my apartment."

"I don't like leaving you," he admitted, and Chloe lit up inside like a sparkler. Then it was doused when he added, "I'd feel better if I made sure you got home safe."

Okay, not that he didn't want to leave her, but his protective instinct to keep her safe was kicking in. Nice, but a little disappointing anyway.

"Don't worry about it," Chloe assured him. "I can take care of myself. You've got things to do and so do I. So, let's do them so we can start the ranching challenge as soon as possible."

He tipped the brim of his hat back, and gave her

a half smile that she'd seen a few times in the last couple of days. And it did what it always did to her— sent licks of flame dancing along her skin.

"You're still set on doing this?" he asked.

A soft, warm wind rushed past them, and Chloe tucked her hair behind her ears. From down the street, a car horn blasted and next door, glass was being swept off the sidewalk.

"Of course. I'm going to prove to you that I can do everything I want those girls to learn," she said.

"All right then." He nodded, though he didn't look convinced. "Let's say you head out to the Perry Ranch in three days. That should give us each enough time to take care of business."

"That works," she said, and held out a hand to him.

He glanced at it and grinned. "Shaking hands now, are we? Thought we'd gotten well past that last night."

Those flames burned hotter now, especially when he took her hand in his and shook it. "Yes, we did," she agreed. "But a handshake on the streets of Houston is probably more acceptable than what we've been doing."

"Not nearly as much fun though," he murmured, and gave her hand one last squeeze before releasing her.

"I'll see you in three days," she said.

"You might regret this," he warned.

No, she wouldn't, Chloe thought. This was the last step she had to take to make her dream come true. But it wasn't just about the camp. This was her chance to live the life she'd always wanted. The little girl she'd once been, dreaming of riding horses and wearing cowboy hats and staring up at a starlit sky, was about to get exactly what she'd wanted. So no, she wouldn't regret it one bit.

But once she passed this test of his, Liam might not be thrilled with the outcome.

"One of us might regret it," she agreed, and smiled.

"You do surprise me, Chloe." He tipped his hat in an old-world gesture of respect, then started walking. "See you soon."

She watched him go, and couldn't quite help the little sigh that slid from her throat. The man had an exceptional butt that deserved a sigh of appreciation. His long legs encased in those worn jeans that stacked up on his brown boots…the too long hair curling from under his dust-brown Stetson. Oh yeah. He was the whole package.

And she couldn't wait to unwrap him again.

Houston had been hit hard, but within twenty-four hours, the city was coming together, cleaning up and clearing out. Online donation accounts had been set up, and the entire state was reaching out to Houston.

Crews were coming from all over Texas and money was pouring into the help fund.

For two days, Chloe performed an amazing juggling act. She spent a lot of time at her ruined office, conducting business on her tablet and phone. Her father, though he disagreed with her life choices, came through for her in the end, hiring a disaster cleanup crew to come in and set it all right. That crew was in demand in the city, but her father made sure she was one of the first people served.

Her landlord had a construction crew in to do a rehab, and she was grateful she wouldn't have to be there while the work was going on. If nothing else, when they were finished, she'd have double-paned windows and floors that didn't creak when you walked on them.

Chloe spent a lot of time online with her clients, reassuring them all that nothing had changed. She was still on top of the events they'd scheduled with her, and assured them that invitations, supplies and reservations were on track. When she could, she spent time helping her neighbors clean up the mess on the street, and by the end of day two she was exhausted.

Through it all though, her mind kept drifting back to Liam. She hadn't heard from him since the afternoon they walked out of the TCC together and went back to their own lives. She missed him. Missed talking to him, laughing with him, missed the sex, a lot.

And she wondered if he was feeling any of this. Or had he been grateful to get back to his real life and leave her behind?

On the third day, when she was sure Houston would move on without her, Chloe packed a bag and headed for the Perry Ranch.

Five days later, she was forced to admit—at least to herself—that ranching was a lot harder than it looked. She'd never been more tired, yet at the same time, she felt a sense of satisfaction she'd never known before. Finally, she was living out what her ten-year-old self had dreamed of.

She'd agreed to Liam's conditions for a couple of reasons—one, she wanted more time with him. Two days in a storm simply weren't enough. But second, she'd wanted to prove to herself that she was up to the task. That she was completely capable of doing the ranching work her father had laughed at her over. And yes, maybe she was trying to prove something to Liam too.

He had a way of looking at her that told her he was half waiting for her to complain about her manicure or about getting dirty or tired. Well, she might have been raised to be a dainty princess, but that wasn't the real Chloe and it was important to her—for reasons she didn't want to think about—that Liam know that. She wanted not only his desire, she wanted his respect. And the only way to get that was to earn it.

Of course, using a pitchfork to clean out a horse's stall wasn't the way she'd have chosen, but at least the double doors at either end of the stable were open to let the breeze slide through, and Chloe was grateful. It was as if that massive storm hadn't happened at all. April in Texas was already hot, steaming toward a blistering summer.

"And speaking of blisters…" She set the pitchfork aside, tore off her left glove and sighed.

"Problem?" Liam walked down the wide aisle to join her.

She jolted, surprised at his appearance. He moved so stealthily sometimes she didn't know he was there until he spoke. Now she turned to look at him. Even in the stable's shadows, those blue eyes of his seemed to burn.

"Nope. No problem." Chloe put her glove back on. She refused to complain about any task he gave her, and she'd be damned if she'd whine about a stupid blister, when she knew darn well that's what he was expecting.

"Let's see it," he said, and grabbed her hand, tugging the leather glove off to inspect her palm. "Yep, that's a big one."

"I'm fine," she said stiffly, desperately trying to disregard the heat pumping through her from the simple touch of his hand on hers.

Since she'd been on the ranch they hadn't been together once. She'd been sleeping in his guest room, catching glimpses of him every night and early in the morning as they passed each other on the way to the coffeepot. He didn't talk so much as grunt. He left her training to Mike, the new foreman, and mostly seemed to be deliberately avoiding being near her.

Chloe could only think that he was regretting what they'd shared during the storm, and that just made her furious. Those two days had been magical for her, and she knew damn well he'd been affected too. But to have him now trying to brush it all aside as if it had never happened made her both sad and livid.

Especially annoying was that just standing this close to Liam had her body humming and her breath shortening into what sounded like gasps even to her. This was humiliating, because apparently Liam was having zero trouble being beside her.

Had he really felt *nothing* during the storm?

"Come on," he said, keeping a tight grip on her hand so she couldn't get away. "There's some ointment in the tack room."

"I'm fine," she argued, trying—and failing—to pull free. "I haven't finished the last stall, and Mike wants them done before dinner."

"Yeah, you're done. One of the boys can finish." He pulled her along behind him, not giving her any choice but to run to keep up. Once inside the tack room, he closed the door behind them and flipped a light on.

There were shutters closed over the single window, giving the place a cave-like feel. It was a small room in the back of the stable, filled with supplies for the horses, and plenty of leather items being repaired. Halters and saddles, she knew, wore out just like anything else, and back here they were repaired or replaced.

It was as tidy as a church, Chloe thought, everything in its place. There were shelves with creams and soaps, and glass-fronted cabinets that held medications. She knew there were plenty of times a rancher would dose his own animals if he knew what the trouble was. For anything serious, the vet would be called out. The room was small, efficient and it smelled like… Liam. Like the outdoors and horses and leather and— Oh, for pity's sake.

Getting a grip on her obviously wayward mind, she said sharply, "I don't need one of 'the boys' to do my work for me."

"That's not what your hands are telling me," he muttered.

Liam let go of her, walked to a heavy wooden cabinet on the far wall and opened it. She tucked her hands behind her back like a child. When she realized it, she let her arms drop to her sides. "I'm doing the work and I don't want help."

"That's too bad," Liam said, glaring at her over his shoulder. "Because you're going to have help anyway."

"I don't take orders well," she told him stiffly.

"You've been taking them from Mike," he reminded her.

"That's different. That's work. I thought I was here to prove myself," she said. "To learn about ranching and to show you that I can do what has to be done."

He grabbed a small tin and palmed it. "You are."

"Well, then let me do it."

"Damn it, Chloe!" He slammed the cabinet door and it crashed shut. Whipping around to glare at her, he shouted, "I didn't bring you out here for you to wear yourself out or to scar and blister yourself."

"For God's sake, a blister isn't fatal."

"Not the point. I don't want you hurt. That's not why you're here," he muttered darkly.

"Why am I here then, Liam? To prove I can make the camp for girls work?" She stared at him and tipped her head to one side. "Or was it because you thought I'd fail, and that way the camp idea would die and you wouldn't be the one killing it."

He snapped a hard look at her. "Where the hell did you come up with that?"

"All on my own," she said. "Believe it or not, I *can* think."

"I didn't say you couldn't, but you're thinking wrongly on this."

"Am I?" she demanded, letting her temper run free after having been bottled up since she got to the ranch and realized how he was going to be treating her. "You've hardly spoken to me in the five days I've been here. I'm staying in your *guest* room, and the only time I see you is at the coffeepot at dawn. Heck, I don't even see you at dinner."

"What did you think was going to happen?" he muttered, flipping the lid off the tin he held.

"Honestly?" she answered frankly. "Sex. I thought sex would happen. A lot of sex."

"Damn it, Chloe…" He tore his hat off, set it aside and stabbed his fingers through his hair.

"Well, why wouldn't I?" Chloe pulled her other glove off and said primly, "We were stranded in the flood and couldn't stop touching each other. Here, we're in the same house, but we might as well be on separate ranches. If you're not interested anymore, just tell me—"

She hadn't heard him move. Hadn't seen him practically jump the distance between them, but all of a sudden, there Liam was, yanking her close. He bent his head and took her mouth with a hunger she hadn't even felt from him the first time they were together.

Chloe wrapped her arms around his neck and hung on, kissing him back with every ounce of need that had been building inside her for days. He kissed her harder, grinding their mouths together while his groin pushed against hers. She felt him, hard, solid, and wanted him more than ever.

When he tore his mouth from hers, she nearly shouted at him to come back. But he took a step to the door, flipped the dead-bolt lock, then was back with her a half second later.

"No interruptions."

"Good idea," Chloe muttered, mouth dry, heartbeat racing. "So I'm guessing you're still interested after all."

His mouth quirked. "You could say so. Damn, Chloe, I've missed you."

"I missed you, too." She cupped his face with her hands. "So get busy already."

"I really like you...."

"Same," Chloe muttered. Then she didn't say one more word when his fingers worked the button fly of her jeans and then pushed them down past her knees. She tried to step out of the damn things, but her boots were in the way and he was touching her, and suddenly she could hardly stand in the wash of sensation pouring through her.

She didn't have to think or do anything to save herself because Liam was there. He pulled her boots off and slid her jeans free, then lifted her and turned for the wall, slamming her back up against it.

"Nice later," he ground out, undoing his jeans and freeing himself. "Fast now."

"Yes," she agreed, and wrapped her legs around his waist. Her gaze locked with his, and she saw the flames in those lake-blue eyes and knew the passion was burning inside her, as well.

He pushed inside her and Chloe gasped at that first, intimate invasion, then gave herself over to the wonder of it. Her mind raced, her pulse jumped into a gallop, her body shook and shuddered with each of his thrusts. What he could do to her should have been illegal, and she was grateful it wasn't. Her head tipped against the wall, she stared blindly at the ceiling as Liam claimed her fast and hard.

Expectation rose up inside her as her body tightened, clenching around his. It had been days since she'd felt this good. This *right*. Trembling, holding her breath, she leaped into the fire and tightened her grip on him as she reached that elusive peak. Chloe bent her head and buried her face in his shoulder, muffling the helpless scream that rattled through her throat as her body shattered.

And what felt like an instant later, Liam groaned through gritted teeth and shuddered in her arms, his body rocking, rocking, as he found the same magic that he'd shown her.

Breathless and achingly aware of just how good it felt to be joined to him, Chloe took a long breath and let it out again. When she lifted her head and looked at him, she whispered, "I'm starting to think of this against-the-wall maneuver as 'our thing.'"

He snorted a laugh and shook his head. "You are

the damnedest woman. I swear I don't understand you at all."

She tipped her head to one side and met his gaze squarely. "So many people say that, and I don't know why. I'm completely upfront about what I want. Why's that hard to understand?"

He lifted her off him, then set her on her own two feet again. While they dressed, he said, "I keep expecting you to be one thing but you're not. Then I forget and you surprise me again."

"That's a lovely thing to say." She liked surprising him. The way his eyes fired when he looked at her always surprised her with a jolt. It was nice to know she could return the favor.

"Figures you'd like that."

"See?" She grinned. "You understand me better than you think you do."

He buttoned his jeans, then walked up to her. "Look, when you got here, I didn't come to you because I didn't want you to think I brought you here for sex."

"Why not?" Shaking her head, she asked, "Did it seem to you that I didn't like what we did in Houston? Why wouldn't I want more of it?"

"Surprised again," he muttered. "Most women would have been pissed that I'd assumed we'd be sharing a bed."

"I'm not most women, Liam," she reminded him.

"And we already shared a bed—and a floor and a wall—so what's the problem?"

He pushed both hands through his hair, and Chloe had begun to recognize it as a move he made when he was giving himself a little extra time to figure out just what he wanted to say. She gave him that time as she struggled to pull her boots on, then stamped her feet into them.

"This isn't going anywhere but a bed, Chloe."

She looked up at him. He'd taken time to think and that's what he'd come up with? "I'm sorry?"

"I'm not looking for a wife."

Chloe shook her head. "I'll make a note."

"Now you're pissed."

"Getting there," she admitted, staring at him. One minute, she was sure he was seeing her for who she really was. And the next, it was clear he didn't. "Liam, I'm not looking for a husband. I'm looking for a campsite. Remember?"

"Not likely to forget that, am I?"

"Well then, stop tacking other things onto what was a simple deal," she said. "I do this for a few weeks, prove to you I'm willing and able, and you give me the land for the camp."

"Yeah…"

He dragged that one word out into about fifteen syllables.

"You know, women are allowed to like sex as much as a man does."

"Oh yeah, believe me I know," he assured her. "And I'm grateful. I just don't want any misunderstandings between us."

"Okay, I give you that," she said. "And it's decent of you to be straight and upfront about how you feel."

He frowned a little.

"That said, I've been upfront too." She trailed her fingertips down the front of his shirt. "I want that camp. That's what I'm concentrating on right now. So I'm here to work. To learn. And, at the end of every day, we get to have sex and there's no strings. For either of us."

"In theory, it sounds perfect," Liam mused as he caught her hand in his. "Like every single man's dream."

"And single woman's, trust me," Chloe told him. "Not every woman needs hearts and flowers to enjoy sex. And we're not all looking for a husband."

He grinned. "Is that right?"

"It is. I'm not looking for promises of forever, Liam, so why don't we both just relax and enjoy what we have, okay?"

"I'll make a note," he said wryly, throwing her words back at her.

Chloe's lips twitched. Honestly, the man touched her on so many levels. He listened when she talked. He smiled at the most intimate moments. He touched her, and she alternately exploded or melted. He made her laugh, made her angry, made her feel so much.

There were too many feelings for Liam Morrow rattling around inside her. He was important to her, but if she told him that right now, he'd go pale and walk away. If she was starting to care more for him than she'd planned on, well, that would remain her little secret. As she'd said, she didn't *need* hearts and flowers, but she was starting to think she'd actually found them without looking.

Shutting down that train of thought fast, she said, "I've got to go finish the stalls."

"Chloe—"

She held up one hand to cut off his argument. "It's my job, Liam, and I can do it."

"Hardheaded woman," he said, shaking his head. "Don't know why I like it so much. Okay, if you're going to do it, give me your hand."

She did, then he picked up the tin of salve he'd tossed onto the desk before their encounter. Carefully, he rubbed a thick, pale ointment onto her palm and the reddening blister. Chloe didn't know which felt better—his touch or that soothing cream. He put her glove back on, looked her directly in the eye and said, "Go on then. I'll see you at the house after work."

She reached up, grabbed the back of his neck and pulled his head down to hers. Then she kissed him, hard and fast, and gave him a wide grin. "That's a date, cowboy."

Seven

She moved into his room that night, and they'd been together ever since. Liam's brain swam with images of how the two of them had spent the last few nights, and his body turned to stone. The woman was going to kill him.

There was still plenty to clean up after that storm. Stock ponds had to be cleared of brush and dirt that had blown in, cattle rounded up from the canyons they'd tried to hide in and three of the cottonwood trees lining the drive had come down in the wind. And that was just the Perry Ranch.

Liam hadn't had a chance to get to his own place in person yet, but he'd spoken to his foreman, Joe

Hardy, every day. They were actually in good shape there. They'd only lost part of a roof on the stable, and a couple of fence lines had gone down when a few dozen cattle made a run for it.

The most disruptive thing caused by the storm was this thing with Chloe. Liam hadn't expected it to go beyond the storm—and why would he? Being trapped together in an emergency was one thing. But in the real world, they were an unlikely pair to say the least.

It wasn't the money thing, because hell, thanks to those ideas he and his friends had come up and then patented in college, Liam probably had more money than Chloe's family now. But he hadn't been raised with inherited wealth or the sense of entitlement that came along with it.

Chloe, on the other hand, was a damn Texas Princess. She might try to deny it, but she was used to nothing but the best. This ranching dream of hers was just that—a dream—and he was pretty sure that as soon as she got tired of it, she'd turn on a dime and run home to daddy. He'd seen it before, after all.

She caught his eye, leading a horse from the stable to the corral. Chloe had a smile on her face that could light up a city, but would it stay? Hell, Tessa had enjoyed simple things too—until she didn't. Then she was gone and Liam had been left standing flat-footed, wondering what the hell had just happened. He didn't intend to go through that again.

Having Chloe here was good and bad as far as he could see. The sex was amazing, but it wasn't a relationship. God, he hated that word. So maybe he was worried about nothing. With Tessa it had been different. He'd let himself believe that what they had would last for the long haul.

This time around, he wasn't kidding himself.

And still when this inevitably ended, he'd miss the damn woman. So no doubt, in letting this whatever it was continue, he was setting himself up for all kinds of misery somewhere down the line. Yet somehow, that knowledge wasn't enough to keep him from her.

The woman made him crazy. Her smiles. Her scent. Her kiss. The way she turned to him in the night, sliding one of her soft, shapely legs across his. Hell, the last few nights had been a damn revelation. Every time he touched her, it only fed the need to touch her again. He couldn't get enough of her, and that was probably not a good thing.

Liam's body was all for this new situation, but his mind kept whispering warnings. Didn't matter what she seemed to be like, he told himself. It was important to remember who she was at the core of her. She was a society woman, born and raised. Whether she fought against that or not, the truth was, she had blue blood and that wasn't going to change.

So he had to remember that this was a physical relationship and nothing more. He couldn't start telling himself she was different. He had to remember that she was going to use him to get what she needed and then she'd move on.

So would he.

"Hey, Liam!"

Grateful for the distraction, he turned toward the shout and saw Mike standing outside the stable, calling, "Looks like Starlight's about to foal. Want me to call the vet?"

One of Sterling Perry's prize mares. Liam started for the stable to check things out for himself. When he got up to Mike, he said, "We'll keep an eye on her. If she's doing well on her own, we won't worry about the vet."

"Right."

Getting back to work was the best way to keep his mind off Chloe, Liam told himself. Maybe he owed that horse a shiny apple for dragging him back to the real world.

The flood had been a gift.

Yes, I felt bad for the people hurt by it, but those rising waters helped me. They still hadn't found it. Maybe they wouldn't. But even if they did, by the time anyone discovered the body, any evidence would have been destroyed by the flood itself.

They would call it murder.

And maybe it was, but I couldn't think about it like that. I hadn't meant to kill him, after all. I was protecting myself. It had to be done. What happened was just self-defense, and wouldn't anyone else have done the same thing?

I was so tired. It felt like my heart weighed a hundred pounds, and it was exhausting just carrying it around. I had been so hurt for so long, it felt like I was born in pain.

None of this was my fault. Someone else started this, I was just finishing it. If things had been different, none of this would have happened.

I wished I could stop dreaming about it, though.

This revenge has been a long time coming, and one day soon, people will know my pain. People will feel what I'd felt for years.

And when they knew the truth, I would finally be free.

If only I could have slept.

"He's beautiful." Chloe leaned her forearms on the top bar of the stall door. Her gaze was locked on the brand-new foal lying in the straw beside his mother.

The quiet was all encompassing. In the middle of the night, the silence was somehow…comforting. Especially since she and Liam were alone in the dimly lit darkness.

She'd been in the stable for hours, helping where she could and so emotionally caught up in the mare's labor, she couldn't have left if someone had ordered her to. Chloe had watched Liam's patience and kindness to the big animal. He'd spent most of the day kneeling in the straw beside the horse, stroking her long, sleek neck when she was distressed and whispering words of comfort, encouragement.

It didn't matter that the mare couldn't possibly understand his words; she knew his gentle touch and the soft tone he used with her. And Chloe had been more deeply touched by it all than she'd ever been by anything else. Liam had simply dropped into her heart and carved out a place for himself.

What that meant she'd worry about later.

"He is a beauty," Liam agreed, mimicking her position at the stall door.

His arm brushed hers, and her stomach dipped and spun. She had to wonder if she would always respond to him like this. She certainly hoped so.

They hadn't had to call the vet after all, and Chloe had been so proud of the mare she had wanted to applaud. Instead, she'd cried when the foal was born and took its first wobbly steps on spindly legs.

"It's silly, but I don't want to leave," she admitted, resting her chin on her crossed arms.

"Not so silly," he said. "I know what you mean."

She turned her head to look up at him. "You get to see this all the time, don't you?"

"I guess so, yeah." He pushed the brim of his ever-present hat back. "But it never gets old."

There was a faint smile on his lips as he watched the new arrival, and Chloe felt as though they were sharing a really special moment. Other men she'd known wouldn't have been interested in the birth of a foal.

Liam was different. In so many ways. He touched her heart as completely as he touched her body. He was stubborn and proud and completely devoted to building the dream he'd been planning for years. And she could understand that, since she was doing the same. In spite of what she'd told him only a few days ago, that she wasn't looking for permanent, Chloe couldn't help but feel that things were changing.

She only wished she knew what to do about that.

Shaking that thought off, she asked abruptly, "Do you have a name for him?"

He gave her a long look. "Not yet. Sterling doesn't really get into naming the animals." He shook his head as if he couldn't believe a man could be that disinterested in his own ranch. "So why don't you do the honors this time?"

Touched and pleased, Chloe smiled. "Really?" She looked back at the tiny black horse with the small white blaze on his forehead. "Okay, how about Shadow?"

Liam thought about it for a moment, then nodded. "Shadow. That's good. I like it."

Chloe let out a happy sigh and turned her gaze back to the new baby. "Welcome to the world, Shadow," she whispered.

The foal dipped his head under his mother's belly to nurse and Liam chuckled, the sound soft and warm in the darkness. "Looks like he doesn't much care what we call him."

"Maybe he doesn't," Chloe said, laying one hand on his forearm. "But I do. This means a lot to me, Liam." She sighed again. "Now I know that even after my time on this ranch is over, a memory of me will still be here."

His eyes darkened like a lake at night. He went perfectly still and then he said, "Yeah. Guess it does mean that."

And, she thought, he didn't look happy about it.

A week later, Liam was still fascinated by her.

She was walking that new foal around like it was a dog and damned if the little animal wasn't following after her like a trusting puppy, too. And even with the extra time she'd been spending with the foal, Chloe worked twice as hard as anyone else and never asked for help. He respected the way she carried her own weight, but he was forced to keep reminding himself that a work ethic didn't mean that she was built for this kind of life.

He couldn't get away from the fact that she hadn't been born with a silver spoon in her mouth, she'd been born with the whole damn set of silver. Her blood was as blue as the Texas sky, and sooner or later, that nature was going to show itself. At some point she'd get tired of being hot and tired. She'd want a manicure and a spa day or whatever it was idle rich women did with their days.

Hell, Tessa had once spent six hours shopping for shoes and hadn't bought a damn thing. It was a way of seeing and being seen, he'd finally figured out. That's what Tessa had been interested in. Being at the right place with the right people at the right time.

And that was Chloe's world, too, despite whatever she was claiming at the moment. He had to remember. Because he wasn't going to allow himself to get dragged back into a relationship that was doomed from the jump.

Just like he and Tessa, Liam and Chloe were from wildly different worlds. He understood his and didn't have a clue about hers.

As if to prove his point, a low-slung, bright red convertible sped up the drive, with a tail of dust streaming up behind it. He tore his gaze from Chloe, who was taking the foal back into the stable, and watched as the car careened around a turn and Tim Logan, one of the ranch hands, did a long jump to avoid being run down.

"Hey, lady! Watch it!" Tim threw a hard look at the woman behind the wheel.

The car came to a sharp stop outside the barn, sending another cloud of dust flying. "Sorry, sorry!" The driver shouted her apology and regally waved one hand at Tim, who cursed under his breath and walked away.

Liam shook his head. He didn't know who she was, but since he'd never seen her here before, he was willing to bet cold hard cash that she had something to do with Chloe.

She seemed to glide out of the car, a beautiful woman in a short, summer blue dress with a full skirt, swinging her bare legs out first. She wore three-inch blue heels, and her light brown hair was like a cloud lifting around her head in the hot breeze.

She slammed the car door, lifted one hand to shield her eyes from the sun and looked around until she spotted Liam. Giving him a well-honed smile, she sashayed toward him. *Sashay* was really the only word that could describe that hip-swaying, deliberately sexual walk. Liam decided that he could like the look of that walk, while at the same time, mentally labeling her as trouble.

"Hi!" She gave him a wide smile that didn't reach her eyes. "I'm Ellen Hemsworth and I'm looking for my sister, Chloe."

"Of course you are," he muttered. Actually, Ellen was exactly what he'd expected Chloe to be, back on that day when he went to have a meeting with her.

"I beg your pardon?" She looked unamused.

Liam's eyebrows lifted. He felt them go and couldn't stop it. This was Chloe's little sister. Driving a car worth more than most men made in a year and looking like she stepped out of a fashion magazine. If he'd needed reinforcement about Chloe and the life she was born to, here it was.

"Is there a problem?" Her tone indicated Queen to Servant, and there was no mistaking it.

"No, ma'am," he said, pointing. "Chloe's in the stable. Right over there."

"The stable?" Ellen grimaced. "Are there horses in there?"

"Yes, ma'am, it's a *stable*," Liam said.

"You're being rude."

"Am I?"

"Do I look like a ma'am to you?"

Liam grinned. "No, ma'am."

She scowled at him. "Stop ma'aming me!"

"Yes, ma'am."

She frowned thoughtfully, but he knew she wasn't thinking about him any longer. Women like her didn't concentrate on anything other than themselves for very long. No doubt she was deciding she didn't want to risk being close to animals if she didn't have to. Then she turned to him again. "Please tell my sister I'm here to see her."

He laughed shortly. She was young and pretty and rich, and probably had never heard the word *no* in her life. He was happy to be the first. "No, ma'am, I won't. I've got work. If you want to see her," he added with a wave of his hand, "just go on in."

Shock etched itself into her features. "Do you know who I am?"

Oddly, Liam was starting to enjoy this encounter. A couple of the guys were angling closer to listen in, and he couldn't blame them. God knew, she was good to look at, but that's where the appeal ended. At the Perry Ranch, there were wealthy guests coming and going all the time. Though not many of them looked like Ellen Hemsworth.

Still, Liam was used to the dismissive glances she was shooting him. And he wondered if she might change her opinion of him if she knew he now had more money than her father. But even if he doubled his current net worth, damned if he'd ever be like the kind of people who'd raised Chloe and her sister.

"Yes, ma'am," he drawled, deliberately sounding slow and stupid. "I do know who you are, since you just told me. Now, if you'll excuse me, I've got work to do." He turned to go, then spotted Chloe stepping into the sunshine from the hidden shadows of the stable. And he saw her expression when she spotted her sister. She didn't look happy.

"Well," he said, deciding to stay right where he was, "there she is now."

"Thank God," Ellen murmured and then shouted, "Chloe! Over here!"

She walked on those ridiculous shoes and wobbled some since the dirt was still a bit sodden from the storm. Liam shook his head and hoped she didn't land on her ass. Not that he cared, but he really didn't want to listen to the screeching complaints.

Chloe hurried over, and instinctively went to hug the woman. Ellen, though, skipped neatly out of reach.

"Chloe, you're filthy!" Ellen's eyes were wide, and her mouth twisted into a grimace.

"I've been working," Chloe said, dusting her hands on the tight, faded jeans she wore nearly every day.

"Doing what for heaven's sake? Rolling in dirt?" Ellen looked her up and down, and Liam almost felt called to defend Chloe.

Hell, she looked beautiful to him. Her skin had a honey-toned glow from her days working in the sun, and even her hair had a couple sun streaks. She wore a short-sleeved, bright blue shirt, those jeans that hugged her legs like an eager lover, and boots that looked a lot more dirty and scarred than they had when she'd arrived more than a week ago.

"Doesn't matter." Chloe sighed, glanced at Liam almost apologetically, then asked her sister, "What are you doing here, Ellen?"

"Oh, I wanted to tell you two things," the woman said, happily bouncing on her toes again. "I'm saving the most important one for last, though. So, Daddy says to tell you your office is all finished."

"Already?" Chloe looked surprised and hell, so was Liam. With so much damage to correct after the storm and the flood, it was amazing that her office had been repaired so quickly.

Ellen sliced one hand in the air, dismissing her sister's surprise. "Daddy offered the crew a big bonus to finish the work fast, and you know how people are. Wave some money at them and they jump for it! Thank goodness, right?"

Liam's eyebrows went up again, and this time they stayed there. One of the cowboys behind him snorted a laugh. He saw Chloe wince a little and knew that though her sister might be clueless, Chloe wasn't. Daddy's checkbook to the rescue. Hell, it was such a cliché it was funny. Damned if Ellen Hemsworth wasn't the walking, talking, poster girl for Texas Princesses.

Even more than that though, for Liam, she was an echoing memory of Tessa. The woman he'd made a damn fool of himself over. It was as if the Universe had reached out to slap him with this living reminder of how badly things had gone the last time he'd tried being with a woman like this one. And standing there listening to Ellen, Liam felt a pang of shame again for letting himself get sucked into Tessa's orbit.

"Okay, thanks for letting me know," Chloe was saying and as she tried to take Ellen's arm to steer her farther away from Liam.

"But I'm not finished. I have more news." She deftly avoided Chloe's hand. "You're dirty. Remember?"

"Fine." Chloe took a deep breath, and sent Liam a look that clearly said, *go away*.

He didn't.

Chloe shook her head, pushed her hair back from her forehead, leaving behind a streak of dirt, and said, "What else did you want to tell me?"

Ellen, too, shot Liam a quick look as if silently ordering him to walk away. He folded his arms across his chest, braced his feet wide apart and let her know he wasn't going anywhere. She frowned, then ignored him again.

"This!" She waved her left hand toward her sister, and displayed a diamond the size of Galveston. "I'm *engaged*! Isn't my ring gorgeous? I swear, he just about knocked me over with this diamond. All my friends are so jealous— Well, Tina would never admit to it, but I saw her eyes go all wide when she saw my ring and I know it's just *killing* her…"

Liam shook his head. The stream of words and the high-pitched tone they were delivered in were like the scratch of nails on a blackboard. Idly, he thought Ellen might be *worse* than Tessa, though once upon a time he would have said that would be impossible.

"I want you to help me find the perfect dress," Ellen ordered, completely ignoring her sister's shocked expression. "You're good at sketching, and I'm actually thinking about designing it myself to be sure it's one of a kind because I don't want anyone else to have a dress like mine, because then it wouldn't even be special. I'm thinking strapless with maybe some lace, and there has to be sequins so the light will catch on me while I walk down the aisle—"

"To who?" Chloe asked.

"What?" Ellen stared at her ring and sighed.

"Who gave you the ring?" Chloe said each word clearly and slowly.

"Oh." Ellen laughed. "Well, Brad, of course. Brad Tracy. You know I've just been crazy for him for six whole months and he's so perfect. Tall and handsome and he looks *so* good in a tux and you know how important that is. He's working for his father in Dallas, so we'll move there after the wedding and his father's going to build us a house in the perfect neighborhood and I get to pick everything out because Brad doesn't care, so…"

"Brad?" Chloe repeated the man's name, and even Liam could hear the distaste in her voice. Ellen, of course, didn't.

"Yes. Brad." Ellen frowned slightly. "Honestly, Chloe, you didn't used to be so slow. It's being out in the sun too much, isn't it? Your skin is just going all brown and that can't be good. Are you wearing sunscreen at all?"

"I'm fine, Ellen," Chloe said tightly. "But you're right. The sun's so hot, you might get burned. You don't want that."

"True, can't risk it. I've got the engagement party Saturday night and—"

Liam was watching Chloe and saw so many different expressions flash across her features and dance in her eyes, it was hard to keep them straight. But the upshot was, she wasn't happy about her sister's engagement.

"Saturday?"

"Didn't I tell you?" She laughed and said, "I know it's short notice, but it's just so wonderful I didn't want to wait. It's just so thrilling, you know? The party, oh, then my shower! You'll have to give it because otherwise Tina will want to and she's just terrible at that sort of thing. Then we have the wedding, the honeymoon… Anyway, the party's at our house. Saturday. Come at eight, okay? You will come, right?"

"Sure," Chloe said when she could slide a word into her sister's stream of consciousness. "I'll be there."

Liam gave silent thanks he wouldn't be.

"Oh, good! And it's black tie of course. I just love the way Brad looks in a tux! Okay then. Better run, have to get a new dress for the party and it's got to be spectacular!" She waved and hurried off to her car, wobbling every step in those heels. Then she was back in her car and careening out of the yard as quickly as she'd come into it.

Silence, blessed silence, descended on them as Liam watched Chloe watching her sister leave. She looked as if she were in shock, and he could completely understand.

"Your sister, huh?" Liam finally said.

"Don't even start," Chloe muttered, and stalked back to the stable.

Eight

They didn't really talk about Ellen's brief but memorable visit. Chloe made it clear the topic was off-limits, and Liam let it go. Maybe her sister visiting had reminded her that she didn't actually belong on a ranch. And if that were the case, then Liam wanted to give her the space and time to let those thoughts settle in.

God knew, Ellen's visit had sent Liam's personal radar screaming. He'd become so used to being with Chloe, to having her in his arms every night and spending every day with her, that he'd allowed himself to forget that this situation was necessarily temporary. Ellen's selfish rant had driven home the truth to him, and he wouldn't be forgetting it again.

By the next morning, Liam was set to drive into Houston. Money and hard donations of clothes, food and water, and paper goods were still pouring in for flood relief. Naturally, Sterling Perry had inserted himself into the middle of it all, because nothing said good publicity like helping out in an emergency. But what that meant was that Liam was in charge of distributing the supplies Sterling had had delivered to the ranch.

But he was looking forward to making the delivery. It would get him off the ranch and away from Chloe for a while—and he needed that space. Even more though, between the flood relief, Chloe and the ranch work here, he still hadn't had a chance to go by his own place to check on it in person. So that was going to be his first stop today. Daily reports from his foreman were good, but Liam wasn't going to relax until he saw the situation for himself.

Checking the load in the back of his truck, he didn't even notice when Chloe and the days-old foal came strolling up. She stopped beside Liam, one hand on the foal's head as the tiny horse leaned into her.

He couldn't have said why the picture they made irritated him. But maybe it was just that she was so much at home on the ranch. She smiled, and he realized that smile was going to haunt him for years. Already, she invaded his dreams, and his thoughts when he should have been concentrating on work. That was worrying. Which was why he needed this break from her so badly.

Liam looked down at the animal before lifting his gaze to hers. "You do realize he's not a poodle, right?"

Affronted, Chloe stroked her hand down the foal's head. "Of course he's not a poodle. He's a big, brave, beautiful horse, isn't he?" At the end, her voice went into baby speak as she cooed to the horse who snuggled even closer to her side.

"For God's sake," Liam muttered, shaking his head. "He's not a pet."

"He's a sweetie and he likes me," Chloe told him, and when he didn't say anything, she asked, "This really bothers you, doesn't it?"

Liam looked at her. Her hair was long and loose, in spite of the heat. She wore figure hugging jeans, and a red T-shirt with a scooped neckline that showed off just the hint of her breasts. And she looked so good, he wanted to strip her right there and lay her out across the hood of the truck just to admire the view.

Well, damn.

He squashed the bubble of frustration in the pit of his stomach, took a deep breath and let it out again. "Not really, no. But you won't be here much longer, so you shouldn't get attached."

* * *

Chloe winced as a sharp pang stabbed at her heart then settled into the center of her chest where it throbbed in time with her pulse. Ridiculous and she knew it. But somehow, being here, working the ranch, living with Liam, a part of her had begun to pretend that it wasn't temporary. That this was her life now.

She'd been keeping up with her event planning business, but her heart really wasn't in it anymore. It was hard to care about monogrammed napkins and silver lace tablecloths when she could be outside working with the horses, talking to the cowboys, riding out with the other hands to inspect the fence line. Life here was real. Immediate. She'd been there for the birth of Shadow, and she'd never experienced anything like that before. It had been… life altering.

In the last couple of weeks, all of the dreams she'd had as a kid had come true. She was living the way she'd always wanted to now, and she didn't want to lose it. Lose *any* of it.

And that included the cowboy who was, at the moment, refusing to look at her. They hadn't really talked since Ellen dropped by the day before, and just remembering her sister's entrance made Chloe groan inwardly. Liam's expression had told her that he'd taken one look at her sister and lumped the two of them together. He saw Chloe as he did her silly, superficial sister—and that hurt.

"Don't get attached," she repeated thoughtfully. "Is that how you do it?"

That got his attention. He snapped his gaze to hers. "Do what?"

"Go from hot to cold so quickly."

"I don't know what you're talking about."

"Wow. That's the first time you've lied to me," Chloe said.

He just looked at her.

"We haven't talked since Ellen was here."

"You made it pretty clear you didn't want to," he pointed out.

"That's fair," she admitted, remembering how embarrassed she'd been by, well, *everything* Ellen had said. "But I'm not like my sister. But then, you should know that already."

"Didn't say you were," he reminded her.

The sun was shining out of a brassy, clear blue sky. Dappled shade from a nearby tree waved across them, but didn't stay long enough to lower the temperature. Even the air was still, as if the Universe was holding its breath, waiting to see how this conversation was going to go.

"Yeah, you didn't have to say it." Chloe swiped her hair off her neck and wished for a clip. "The fact that you're not talking to me—is that your way of not getting attached?"

He straightened up, tugged his hat brim down until his lake-blue eyes were partially hidden from her. To protect himself? Or her?

"There is no attachment, Chloe," he said, keeping his voice low. "There won't be, either. We agreed to that when this whole thing started up."

Her heart took another hit, but she fought past it to say, "We did. But sometimes things change." They had for her, anyway. This man had crept into her heart, her soul, her mind. It felt as if he were a part of her now, and ripping him out just might kill her.

"And sometimes they don't." His voice was still low, but clipped as if letting her know he wasn't going to discuss this much longer.

"And sometimes they do and we just pretend they don't," Chloe said.

He narrowed his eyes on her, and she met his steady gaze without flinching. Humming tension stretched out between them, as if it were an actual, electrical cord arcing back and forth. Seconds passed, and the only sounds were from the cowboys in the corral and snuffling from the tiny horse.

Finally, Liam simply said, "I've got to get going."

Moment shattered, Chloe stopped him by asking, "Where are you taking this load?"

"To the shelter in Houston," he said shortly, and knotted the rope holding the white tarp down over the donated supplies.

She smiled to herself. Perfect. If she went with

him, they'd have some time. Time to talk. To figure out what they were doing and where they were going—if anywhere.

"I'll ride with you," she said, and his head snapped up.

"Yeah, I don't think so. You've got work here, remember? Learning ranching, following Mike around?"

"Oh, I know." Chloe stroked one hand across the top of Shadow's head and smiled as she shrugged. "But Mike's taking the day to go with his wife to visit her family, so he said I could take the day too."

He didn't look happy about that, Chloe thought, but that was all right. It meant he wasn't as unaffected by her as he was trying to pretend.

"I don't think it's a good idea." He checked the ties on the tarp.

"Why not?"

He scowled at her. "Because I'm stopping by my place on the way," he said. "I need to see it for myself. Make sure everything's all right after the storm."

"What a great idea!" She grinned and added, "I'd love to see your ranch. After all, if I pass your test, that's where the camp will be."

Shaking his head, Liam muttered, "I'm not getting rid of you today, am I?"

"Doesn't look like it," she said, still smiling.

Frowning, he thought about it for a second or two, and Chloe was glad she couldn't read his mind.

"Fine," he said. "If you're coming…" He whistled, a sharp, clear sound and caught Tim Logan's attention. The cowboy ran over and Liam said, "Take Shadow back to his mother, will you, Tim?"

"Sure thing, boss."

"I'll see you later, Shadow," Chloe said, and bent to kiss the tiny horse's forehead.

"Oh for—" Liam bit back the rest of that sentence, but she didn't need to be told how it would have ended.

She climbed into the passenger seat of his truck, and caught him watching her as she buckled her seat belt. "Are we going or not?"

"Yeah." He slammed the passenger door, and Chloe hid a smile as he stomped around the front of the truck and got in behind the wheel. He fired up the engine, shot her a telling glance and ground out, "Looks like we're both going."

Liam's ranch was beautiful.

Chloe loved it at first sight.

Texas live oaks dotted the yard and were almost a part of the house itself. Liam hadn't torn them out to build. Instead, his house had been constructed around them. The home itself, unlike Sterling Perry's massive, glittering white mansion, was a sprawling, two story building with a wide porch that snaked along the outside of the structure. The walls were wood logs and river stones, and the roof was cedar shakes that gave it a mountain cabin look.

But it was so much more than a cabin. It was warm, welcoming and was laid out in a jigsaw pattern, she thought as she looked at it, to snake around the oaks that shaded the roof against the hot Texas sun.

"I love this," she whispered. Turning to look at him as he shut off the engine, she said, "It's beautiful. I love that you left the trees."

He shrugged, but his expression said plainly that he was pleased with the compliment. "Those trees have been here longer than I have."

"Most people would have ripped them out," she said, turning to look at the house again. She could see two stone patios, created by the house circling one or more trees. Those patios held wooden tables, and chairs with bright cushions, and in the shade of the oaks, they looked like tiny oases.

Liam got out of the truck and Chloe did the same. While he strode across the ranch yard toward a much shorter man hurrying up to him, she looked around. There wasn't much evidence of storm damage here. It looked like a few of the trees had lost some branches, and the ground beneath her boots was still soft and sodden from all the rain. But otherwise, everything about this place was perfect.

It wasn't just the house that was impressive,

though. The whole ranch was laid out carefully, with a big corral, a stable and a huge barn. There were outbuildings, bunkhouses probably for the single cowboys and two smaller houses, one of which was no doubt for his foreman. The corral fence was painted a gleaming white, while the barn and the huge stable were painted brick red with white trim.

While Liam talked to the man she assumed was his foreman, Chloe turned in a slow circle taking it all in. The land itself was gorgeous, trees, meadows and in the distance, the silvery shine of water in a stock pond. It was quiet, but for the wind in the trees, the horses in the corral and what sounded like a chorus of birds.

If everything went as well as she hoped it would, her girls' camp would be here. She took a deep breath and looked to the far side of the house. That, she told herself, was where she would put her cowgirl camp. If nothing else, she had to have convinced Liam by now that she could do the work. That she had been made for this kind of life.

"You've got a planning gleam in your eyes."

"What?" She jumped, and glanced over to see Liam had walked up beside her and she hadn't noticed. "You know, I'm starting to think you walk that quietly on purpose because you enjoy seeing me jolt."

He shrugged. "Maybe that's just a bonus."

Well, at least he wasn't irritated anymore. She pointed to where oaks, gathered together on gnarled trunks, formed a circle, as if just waiting for a group of girls to hold a campfire.

"I'd want to put the camp there. Close to the house but far enough away to ensure your privacy, too."

"Decent of you," he muttered.

Well, that sounded like regret. She looked at him. "You did say you'd give me the land for the camp if I proved myself."

"I did." He pulled his hat off and stabbed his fingers through his hair. "But that hasn't happened yet, so don't get ahead of yourself."

The dismissiveness in his tone surprised her. Disappointed her. "Huh. The last two weeks mean nothing, do they? I haven't proven myself to you. You still expect me to fail, don't you?"

He took a breath, met her eyes and said, "Not expect so much as… Okay, yeah. I do."

Slowly, carefully, she plucked windblown hair from her eyes, giving herself an extra moment or two to accept what he'd said. But it didn't matter. She couldn't accept it. Never would.

"Why?"

"You're not built for this life, Chloe, plain and simple."

"What am I built for then?" she demanded, and crossed her arms over her chest. "Shopping? Nightclubs? High tea with the dowager Queens of Houston?"

He threw both hands up. "How the hell do I know what you were made for?"

"You should know," she accused, stepping into his space, fighting past the pain and instead reaching for righteous fury. "You more than anyone. You know what this means to me. You know how hard I've worked to prove myself."

"Yeah, I do," he said tightly. "But I have to look at more than that."

"Really?" Her throat felt dangerously tight. She didn't want emotions crowding this argument, so she fought past the hurt, the disappointment and clung to the fury. "What else is there, Liam? What hidden tests have I been failing?"

The minute she said it, she *knew*. "This is about my sister, isn't it?"

He looked as though he might deny it, but then he nodded. "Partly, yeah. Hell, Chloe, you come from the same life that made *her*. And she could no more survive at ranching than I could trying to breathe underwater."

Insult now mingled with her rage. "That works out well for Ellen, since she has no desire to live or work on a ranch. The difference is, I do. I walked away from that life, remember?"

He snorted and shook his head. "You may have, but that life hasn't left you. The whole damn city of Houston is looking to rebuild, but your rich daddy swooped in and made sure your office was fixed first."

"Seriously?" Eyes wide, she stared at him, stupefied. "It's my fault that my father overpaid a construction crew to get work done in a hurry?"

"No, it's not. But I notice you didn't tell him not to do it."

"You're right." Nodding sharply, she said, "I should have insisted on going to the back of the line. Heck, I shouldn't have let them repair the building at all. I should have worked in a hovel to make sure I passed your 'poor but proud' test."

"Here now," he countered.

"Oh no, my turn." She whirled around, took two or three long strides away from him, then came right back again. Shaking her index finger at him, she said, "You know what's wrong with you, Liam? It's amazing I never caught it before today. Oh, I noticed stubborn. Cranky. But this one slipped past me. The truth is, you're a snob."

His eyebrows arched high on his forehead. "Excuse me?"

"The worst kind, too," she said. "A reverse snob. You're so busy looking down on people with money, you don't give them credit for being people at all."

"That's not true."

"Really?" She tapped the toe of her boot against the grass and folded her arms over her chest. "Sterling drives you crazy. You met my sister for five minutes and dismissed her."

"She's ridiculous," he argued.

"Maybe, but you don't get to make that judgment based on listening to one conversation."

"One was enough," he said fervently.

"And worst of all," she went on as if he hadn't spoken, "you had me failing before this experiment even began, didn't you?"

He shook his head. "I gave you a fair chance."

"A chance, anyway. Hardly fair. Not if you already had me judged before I began."

"I told you I thought you'd done a good job so far."

"Aha!" She stabbed the air with her finger. "So far. Leaving me plenty of room to fail."

"Look," he said, clearly irritated, "you can't blame me for making judgments. I've known plenty of women like your sister, and you come from the same crop, so to speak. Why should I believe you're different?"

"Oh, I don't know. Open your eyes, maybe?" This was just infuriating. Chloe was trembling with waves of indignation. Her whole life, she'd been the outsider in her family. The one who didn't fit in. Didn't belong. Now she found the place she wanted to be and still she didn't belong. "Haven't I done everything you and Mike have asked of me?"

"Yeah, you have." He pulled his hat back on and lowered the brim over his eyes.

"I've mucked out stalls, fed cattle, fixed fencing, all without a complaint." And she was damn proud of it.

"You have," he admitted, and folded his arms across his chest too. Now they stood like bookends, facing each other, neither of them giving an inch.

"So if that's all true, why do you still think I'll fail?"

"Because you've been doing it for a couple weeks. Once the newness wears off, things will change."

"Because I don't care about my dreams as much as you did about yours?"

His lips twisted into a frown. "Dreams have nothing to do with this."

"Of course they do!" She swept her arms out, encompassing the beautiful ranch. The life he'd built for himself because he'd dreamed it and made it happen. "This is what you did because of your dreams."

"And it took me years, not weeks."

"And that makes a difference?"

"It does," he snapped. "When something comes easy, you don't appreciate it as much."

"Easy?" Hurt tangled in her chest, squeezed her heart and made her sound breathless. "I've been working my whole life to carve out what I want for myself. I've stepped away from my family's expectations and started my own path, and you call that easy? My God, who do you think you are, anyway?"

"I know exactly who I am, Chloe," he said softly. "It's you I'm not so sure about."

Another slap and this time she nearly staggered. She'd thought they had a connection. That they'd forged a bond of some sort during the two days they were trapped together during the storm. Since then, they'd built on that, or so she'd thought. These last couple of weeks at the Perry Ranch, Chloe had believed she'd earned his respect if nothing else, but apparently she'd been fooling herself.

"*Easy*," she repeated, her voice a low throb of hurt and insult. "That's what you said, right? That I would get my dream too easily?"

"Chloe—"

"You once said you admired how I went after my dream, do you remember?"

"Yeah, I do." He shoved his hands into his jeans pockets.

"I've held up my end of our bargain, haven't I?"

"Yes."

"I've got what, another week to go?"

"About that."

"Fine." She breathed deep, drawing in enough air to feed the fire burning deep in her gut. "When the time's up, you're going to have to admit that I won."

"It's not a contest, Chloe," he said tightly.

"Oh, yes it is." She shook her hair back, lifted her chin and locked her gaze with his. "All my life, people have been telling me no, you can't, you won't.

Well, every time they said it, the words only fired my determination to prove them wrong. This time won't be any different."

"Damn it, Chloe—"

"And as for the 'newness' wearing off..." she continued, cutting him off neatly. "Well, you don't have to worry about that. I pass your test, I get the land. That was our deal."

"I know what the damn deal was."

"Good. Just make sure you honor it."

"I don't go back on my word," he said, sounding as insulted as she felt.

"Well, how can I be sure? Turns out I don't really know you, either."

Two days later, Liam was a man on edge. And walking across the yard to a meeting with Sterling wasn't improving his mood any.

Since their confrontation at his ranch, he and Chloe had hardly spoken. She'd moved out of his room and back to the guest bedroom, and that was eating at him. Probably for the best, he kept telling himself, though his dick didn't believe him.

And it was more than the sex he missed, damn it.

He liked waking up with her snuggled against him. Liked how she smiled at him when she first opened her eyes. Liked the way she sang in the shower. Liked too damn much about her, really.

But memories of her sister crowded into his brain

and reminded him that Chloe was no different at the core of it. How could he trust her when a part of him was waiting for her to become who she was born to be?

Nine

"I need you to do something for me this Saturday." Sterling Perry leaned back in his chair and tapped his fingers on the desktop.

Liam slapped his hat against his thigh. Impatient, he'd been making small talk with Sterling for a few minutes now. He was supposed to meet Mike out on the range, show him the canyons where the herd was most likely to wander. Instead, he was standing here, waiting for Sterling to get to the point. God, he was looking forward to being at his own place.

He liked Sterling fine, but the man had a way of stalling, dragging things out that drove Liam nuts. "Yeah, so you said earlier. What've you got in mind?"

"Simple," his boss said. "I was invited to an engagement party for your girl Chloe's younger sister."

Liam stiffened. Cagey as ever, Sterling noticed plenty even if he was rarely out and about on the ranch. Somehow, he'd picked up on what was between Liam and Chloe. "She's not my girl. Not anybody's *girl*. She's a woman."

Nodding, Sterling said with some amusement, "So you did notice."

Oh, he'd noticed all right. Not that it was any of his boss' concern. "Sterling—"

The older man shook his head and held up one finger for silence. "Not my point. What you do on your own time is your business. But her father is something else again. Hemsworth is a client. I should be represented there, but I've no interest in going."

Liam scowled. "Neither do I."

Sterling actually laughed. "Yes, I know. But you're still my foreman and I need you to be there, representing me and the ranch."

This wasn't the first time Sterling had thrown a curveball at Liam. He'd stood in for the older man at meetings, at the new TCC, at horse auctions and now, it seemed, at an engagement party. Well, he wasn't going to surrender without a fight. Hell, he'd met Ellen Hemsworth for five minutes and couldn't stand her. Not to mention that Chloe would be there and he was, at the moment, actively avoiding her.

"Damn it, going to parties isn't part of my job."

There was nothing he wanted to do less than go to that particular celebration. Hell, it sounded like torture. Mingling with the rich and useless. Making small talk with people he didn't give a damn about. Plus, it was black tie. Wearing a damn tux all night?

"It is now," Sterling said flatly. "You represent the Perry Ranch at the party, Liam. We keep our clients happy."

"Send Mike," Liam said, grasping for any straw at all. The fact that it meant he was throwing a friend under the bus didn't bother him in this case, either. "He's your new foreman. He should get used to dealing with this stuff."

Even at seventy, Sterling Perry was an intimidating figure. His brown hair was graying at the temples, but that was the only sign that he'd surrendered to the years. Liam waited for the man to respond, even though he was pretty sure what he'd have to say. He wasn't wrong.

Sterling frowned. "Mike Hagen isn't foreman until you've completed your debt to me, Liam. You're almost clear of it, so just do your job when I tell you to do it and we won't have a problem."

Liam was caught and he knew it. He'd given his word to work off his debt to Sterling, and until the old man told him it was paid in full, Liam didn't have a choice. Which the cagey old bastard knew.

When Sterling picked up the phone and started dialing, the dismissal was apparent. Liam had to swallow back his anger. There'd be no argument here. Sterling ran his ranch like a kingdom, and like any good king, he didn't take any crap from the peasants.

So it looked like Liam was going to a party.

Frustrated, angry and ready to bite someone's head off, Liam stomped out of the office and got half-way down the hall before Esme Perry stopped him.

"Wow, Dad has quite the effect on you."

He turned his head To look at her. "Not in the mood, Esme."

"This about the big engagement party?"

"You know about it?" He turned to watch her stroll down the staircase as she had the last time he'd had a meeting with Sterling. The one that had gotten him into this whole mess. "Do you actually lurk on the staircase waiting for me to get in a fight with your father?"

She laughed a little. "Believe me, I have better things to do. As for this party, everybody knows about it. Supposed to be a big event. The Hemsworths aren't known for their subtlety."

"Great. Are you going?" he asked, thinking if she was, then he didn't have to. Who better to represent the Perrys than one of them?

"Oh, hell no," she said, laughing. "It's all on you, Liam. You're the representative this time."

"Lucky me."

"No, lucky *me*," she said. "Ellen Hemsworth is a silly twit. She gives me a headache."

"She's a piece of work all right," he muttered, remembering the woman hopping up and down waving a gigantic diamond in the air. Then he remembered Chloe standing there in her jeans and boots, looking and acting nothing like her sister.

"Thank God all Chloe shares with Ellen is a last name," Esme said, as if reading his mind. "She's smart. Capable."

"Yeah," he murmured reluctantly. "She is."

"I like her."

He heard the curiosity in her tone. Liam shot her a look. "Is there a point to this?"

"Do I need one?" Esme laughed and shook her hair back from her face. "Honestly, Liam, I'm not blind. And I do live here. I've seen the two of you together, and you look pretty cozy to me."

Liam shouldn't have been surprised that people at the ranch—Esme and her father included—had noticed he and Chloe spending time together. But it irritated him just the same.

"People pay too much attention to things that aren't their own business."

"Probably, but where's the fun in minding my own?" She came down the last of the stairs and looked up at him. The amusement on her features faded away at the look in his eyes. "Trouble in paradise?"

He glared at her. They might be friends, but he wasn't the kind of man to talk out his problems and have someone pat his head. He didn't do "sharing."

"Leave it alone, Esme."

"God, you're a stubborn man," she said with a sigh. "Okay, fine. No more talk about Chloe. Back to the party. Just relax about it, Liam. You're almost finished here at the ranch. What's one more event? You've only got what? One week left?"

"Little less."

She smiled. "Well then, you'll soon be free."

"Yeah, guess I will," he said.

As free as he could be with Chloe's camp at his ranch and him having to see her at least once a month. He didn't know what the hell he'd been thinking, offering up his ranch for her cowgirl camp. If he hadn't, she'd have set up shop here at Sterling's place and he wouldn't have had to see her again.

And he suddenly didn't know what would be worse. Seeing her a lot. Or never seeing her again. Hell, there was just no way to win here.

So she'd have her camp and they'd be...strangers who'd seen each other naked. No problem.

"Now that's interesting," Esme mused, tapping one finger against her bottom lip.

"What?" Wary, he gave her a hard look.

"Well, for a soon to be free man, you don't look real happy about it."

"I'm plenty happy," he snapped.

"Yes," she said with a grin as her eyebrows lifted. "I can hear that in your carefree tone."

She stood there, looking cool and pretty and amused, and that just fried Liam's ass. Friend or no friend, he wasn't going to be her entertainment for the day.

"Damn it, Esme, I've got work to do," he ground out, then stalked down the entry way and out the front door, Esme's laughter following after him.

He needed some damn air.

Chloe was bored to tears.

Her sister's engagement party was like every formal event Chloe had ever attended. And it proved why she'd always hated them. It was crowded, noisy and sure to make her want to run away in under an hour. She'd been there only forty-five minutes and she'd started checking out the closest exit. No one would even notice she was gone. Since she was in the big backyard with most of the crowd, all she'd have to do was slip out the side gate and get one of the valets to bring her car around.

Then she sighed. She wasn't going to run and she knew it, in spite of how much fun it was to plan her escape. Having family wasn't always easy. Ellen was silly, too young to get married and in no way ready to be an adult, but she was also Chloe's sister, so here Chloe would stay. She just hoped the waiters kept the champagne coming.

The band was tucked into a corner near the custom patio, playing classics from her father's generation. There were a few couples dancing, but most people were huddled in groups, lost in conversations that seemed to ebb and flow around her like waves on the ocean.

Chloe took a sip of champagne and looked at the party through the critical eyes of an event planner. There were twinkling white fairy lights strung in the trees and across the open spaces. Tables and chairs were set up haphazardly, and waiters wandered the yard offering trays of canapés and drinks.

If she'd been designing the party, Chloe would have arranged the tables in a half circle, giving dancers more room to move. The lights wouldn't have been twinkling, and the waiters would know to crisscross the yard to make sure everyone was covered.

But her father hadn't bothered to ask her to organize the event. Mostly, she thought, because he didn't want to help her be a success. He wanted her to fail spectacularly so she'd fall back into line with his plans for her life. He'd had her office fixed so quickly, because how could she fail if she didn't have an office to work from? Besides, what would people think if Chloe's father allowed her to work in some dismal, dank building? Oh, she knew how her father thought. What he expected of her and she knew that part of his disgust with her "little" business was the idea of her making customers out of his friends. Working for people he socialized with.

"And, this is getting you nowhere, Chloe," she

murmured and took another sip of champagne. She'd give the party another hour, and then she'd leave. Go back to the Perry Ranch. Back to the house where she and Liam were living like strangers.

Chloe stared across the manicured back lawn to where her sister and Brad were accepting congratulations from the adoring crowd. At least Ellen looked happy. Chloe hoped this marriage would work out, and maybe it would. The happy couple wanted the same things, after all. Prestige and pretty lives.

As her own heart was aching, she thought that maybe it was better to live Ellen's way. Don't expect too much and then you're never disappointed. But you were never really happy, either. So did you risk the hurt for the chance at happiness? Or was it better to just take what was offered and convince yourself you were satisfied?

Another sip of champagne and she pushed her thoughts aside. She'd have lots of time to consider what she'd done or should have done. Years. Because she couldn't imagine ever feeling for anyone else what she did for Liam. How could she try to find love with someone else when her heart would always be with him?

"Looks like some dark thoughts for a party."

She jolted and looked up into Liam's lake-blue eyes. She hadn't heard him approach. Again. "You know, being stealthy is really annoying."

He gave her a half smile. "I'll work on that."

God, he looked wonderful. Black dress Stetson, a tux that had clearly been tailored to fit his muscled, rangy body and gleaming black boots. He looked the image of every romantic cowboy fantasy. And he was staring at her as if he wanted to take a bite.

She shivered and wished he would.

"What're you doing here, Liam?"

"Sterling sent me as his representative," he said, glancing around the massive yard and all the people gathered there. When he looked back at her, his gaze swept her up and down.

Chloe's blood heated in response, and she had one quick moment to be grateful she'd gone shopping especially for the party. Her dress was midnight blue silk, shot through with silver threads. It clung to her body and fell straight to the floor. There was a side slit that went high on her right thigh, and the bodice was cut low and supported by two slim straps over her shoulders. The back was a deep vee, and the soft Texas air caressed her skin as she stood there with his eyes on her.

"You look…beautiful."

His voice was soft, almost lost in the surrounding noise of dozens of conversations.

"Thank you. You look amazing." Just honest, she thought, enjoying the sight of him in that elegant tuxedo. The black Stetson he wore only added to the whole picture.

Nodding, he mused, "Seems like a nice party."

She laughed and shook her head. "You hate it."

"True," he said with a shrug, "but it seems nice enough."

"Honestly, I'm bored to tears," she admitted, letting her gaze slide around the lawn. "I'm here for Ellen, though I don't think she's even noticed me yet."

"I don't know how she could miss you."

Chloe slid her gaze to his and saw passion glittering in the depths of his eyes. Her body stirred in response, but her heart ached, because passion wasn't enough anymore.

For the last few days, she'd been struggling with a hard truth that had somehow slipped up on her. She was falling in love with this hardheaded cowboy. A man who didn't respect her abilities. Who thought because she was a rich man's daughter, she was incapable of being more.

And that broke her heart.

"I don't think I like what I'm seeing in your eyes," he said. A waiter stopped to offer a tray of champagne flutes, but Liam waved him off.

"What is it you think you see?"

Frowning, he said, "In a word, disappointment."

"Good catch." Strange that he could see that in her eyes, but he couldn't see the love she had for him. A loose strand of hair fell from the messy bun knotted at the back of her head and impatiently, she tucked it behind her ear. "Liam—"

"You're wrong," he said quietly.

Curious, she asked, "About what?"

He inhaled sharply. "About what I think of you."

Sadly, she wasn't. "Oh, I think you were pretty clear the other day."

"I was pissed," he confessed. "Said some things I shouldn't have."

Stunned, she stared up at him. "If that's an apology, it's not very good," she told him.

"Yeah, it's not an apology."

"Oh, great. Well, thanks for stopping by." Chloe looked across the yard and watched her little sister throw herself into Brad's arms.

Whatever Chloe might think of Ellen's upcoming marriage, at least her sister had found someone who loved her. That put her miles ahead of Chloe.

"Here's something I haven't told you enough," he said softly. "You've done a hell of a job, Chloe."

She turned her head to look at him. "Is that right?"

"It is. You stood up and I didn't think you could. You did the work and didn't bitch about it."

"That's practically Shakespeare, Liam." Her lips twitched. He wouldn't apologize, but he would compliment her, however grudgingly.

He smiled, and the action sent ripples of heat rushing through her. "If that's how you feel, then what's the problem?" she asked him.

That smile faded. "A lot of stuff I really don't want to talk about."

"That doesn't help me, Liam."

"Yeah. I know." Clearly irritated, he pulled his hat off, slapped it against his thigh. "I can't help that. But damn it, Chloe, we've got a few days left of this bargain. You really want to spend them fighting?"

Well, he had her there. No, she didn't want to fight with him anymore. She hated being in the guest room. Hated not talking to him, not feeling his arms come around her. Hated waking up and reaching across an empty bed for him.

He was watching her. Waiting. She could feel the tension between them like a pounding heartbeat. He was right. In a few days, this bargain would be done, and who knew what would happen then? Did she really want to cheat herself out of whatever time she had left with him?

"No," she said finally, going with her heart. If she listened to her head, it would tell her that nothing could be solved by pretending everything was all right. But that wasn't what she wanted to hear.

"Thank God." He grabbed her hand and pulled her in close.

She laughed a little and asked, "Are we going to dance?"

"Not in this lifetime. I don't dance." But he held her as if they were dancing and turned in a slow circle beneath the white fairy lights. And as the light and shadow played across his features, Chloe took that last slide into love.

In that moment she knew, however their bargain ended, nothing would ever be the same for her again.

Back at his cabin, they walked into his bedroom together, darkness shattered only by the moonlight streaming through the windows. Liam closed the door behind them, then turned to her. He slid the straps of her gown off her shoulders and pushed the bodice down, exposing her breasts to the coolness of the room. Her nipples hardened and he smiled.

"I've missed the taste of you," he whispered, and bent to take first one nipple then the other into his mouth. Chloe stood there, hands on his shoulders to maintain her balance, while the world tipped around her. His lips and tongue and teeth worked her flesh, sending her mind into a tailspin while it handed over control to her body.

"Liam," she said on a groan, "I'm going to fall over in a minute."

He straightened up, looked down into her eyes and said, "I can fix that." Sweeping her up in his arms, he carried her to the bed and laid her down on the mattress. "Just stay right there."

There was nowhere else she wanted to be, Chloe thought, running her own hands up and down her torso, cupping her breasts while he watched her through hungry eyes. He tore off his tuxedo jacket, tie and shirt, then knelt in front of her and pulled her hips to the edge of the bed.

"Liam?"

"Like I said," he whispered, "I missed the taste of you."

He flipped her midnight silk gown out of the way and smiled when he realized she hadn't been wearing underwear. "Well now, if I'd known this, we might not have made it back to the cabin."

She smiled. "I didn't want any lines to show under my dress."

"Well, I'm a big fan of fashion, then." His thumb stroked that teardrop birthmark on the inside of her right thigh, then moved higher, closer to the burning, throbbing core of her.

Chloe held her breath and parted her thighs for him. Expectation roared into life inside her, and her breath staggered in her lungs.

He stroked her heat, dipped his fingers into her depths, then caressed her again. And Chloe writhed on the mattress, need building, desire pumping through her system. Helplessly, she rocked her hips, wanting, waiting. Liam kissed his way up her thigh, licking that birthmark that seemed to fascinate him so. And then finally, finally, he took her the way she wanted to be taken.

His mouth covered her, his tongue stroked her folds and his hot breath brushed across her own heat and set a blaze that threatened to consume her. Chloe twisted in his grasp as if trying to escape when she was really trying to get even closer, feel even more.

Reaching down, she threaded her fingers through his hair and held his head to her. Letting him know, without speaking, that she loved what he was doing to her. That she never wanted it to end.

She looked down at him and watched him taking her so intimately, and that only fed those dancing flames within. Chloe shifted, moved, rocked, all to ratchet up the expectation and the tightening coil of pleasure inside. Again and again, he licked her, nibbled at her, then he slipped one finger inside her and the combination was just too much for her.

She couldn't hold on a moment longer, couldn't stretch out the pleasure for a second more. When her climax hit, Chloe screamed his name and shuddered with the force of the release shaking her. It seemed to go on and on, and she rode those endless waves with a whimpering shiver.

Liam stood, shucked the rest of his clothes and was on her in an instant. He pushed his body deeply within hers while she was still trembling. Chloe wouldn't have thought it possible for her to climax again so quickly, but Liam made everything possible.

She wrapped her legs around his hips, taking him as deeply as possible. He looked down into her eyes and she read the hunger there. She matched it, needing him more even than she had a moment ago. With sure, purposeful strokes, he claimed her, pushing her higher and higher until finally, her body exploded again, and this time she took him with her. While she held him close, while they were linked so intimately, they plunged into the shadows and made them shine.

After a long, satisfying night of sex, Chloe woke up wrapped in Liam's arms, and just for a moment, she paused to savor it. As wonderful as the night had been, she knew that nothing between them had been solved. Nothing had been talked out or decided.

As intimate as they were, as closely joined, Liam was holding back from her and she didn't know why.

"I can hear you thinking," he murmured.

"Yeah." She glanced out the window to where dawn was just streaking the sky with shades of rose and gold. Soon they'd be up and working, each of them doing what they were supposed to do, neither of them talking about what they were *going* to do.

And she couldn't stand it.

Pushing away from him, she went up on one elbow to look down into his eyes. "What's happening here, Liam?"

He reached to tuck her hair behind her ear. "We had a great night and now it's morning."

"Don't do that," she said, shaking her head. "That's not what I meant and you know it. I want to know what's happening between us." Cupping his cheek with her palm, she said, "I'm not talking about the camp or the ranch or anything else. Just us."

He sighed and rolled out of bed. "I'm not doing this now, Chloe."

"The problem is, you never want to do it."

Liam glanced at her over his shoulder. "And yet you keep pushing."

"Of course I do, Liam. I want to *know*." Her gaze swept over his hard, tanned body. She knew every line, every scar. And yet, there was so much locked inside him that he was keeping from her.

"Maybe you don't." The words were enigmatic and only served to feed her need to hear the truth.

Sitting up, she tugged the sheet high enough to cover her breasts. "Why not? Like you said, we've only got a few days left in this bargain, so let's at least have honesty between us."

He grabbed a pair of jeans and yanked them on, not bothering to do up the button fly. His hair was too long, and he shoved it back from his face. "What part of 'I don't want to talk about this' do you not get?"

"All of it," she countered. "What part of 'talk to me anyway,' do you not get?"

He fired a hard look at her, then stomped out of the room. She knew he was headed for the kitchen. For coffee. So she grabbed his dress shirt from the night before, pulled it on and followed him.

He was standing at the sink, staring out at the ranch and gulping that coffee like it was the only thing keeping him alive. He didn't even glance at her when she walked into the room. Chloe poured herself a cup of coffee because going into a confrontation without it was just unthinkable. And judging from the set of his shoulders and the hard line of his jaw, this was going to be a battle.

"Tell me," she demanded. "There's more going on here than just an issue with me. So why don't you start with why you hate the wealthy so much. You're rich, too, remember?"

He slanted her a long look. "I worked for my money."

Taken completely aback, she stared at him. "And no one else did?"

"Not the same," he said tightly.

"Then explain it."

"Fine." He turned around, braced one hip against the edge of the counter and looked at her over the rim of his coffee mug. "You were born into money. Your father, too, probably."

"And that's bad." It wasn't a question, because she could see in his eyes that he definitely thought it was a bad thing.

"Not bad. Just easy. You can't appreciate something if you never had to work for it." He set his cup down. "I saw those people at the party last night. The women dripping in diamonds and the men standing around bragging to each other about their country clubs or cars or golf scores or whatever the hell else they care about. No one was talking about work."

"It was a *party*," Chloe said, and felt the first wave

of frustration rise up to nearly choke her. "People were there to have a good time."

"And to show off."

He had a point, but... "For some people that *is* the good time."

He snorted and shook his head.

And still she tried to break through whatever wall of silence he'd erected around himself. What they had was ending, and she at least deserved to know why.

"I'm not going to apologize for my family. I've already told you that I left that life as soon as I could. I work for a living, remember?"

"For now," he acknowledged.

Those two words hit a trip wire inside Chloe. She felt the physical snap of the leash holding her temper back. "How do you get to make proclamations about what I'm going to do with my life?"

He snapped her a fiery look, and she knew that he too had reached the point where the truth would spill out or be buried forever. "I've seen it before."

"With who?"

"A woman like you," he said. "Born to money. Beautiful. Building her own life, she said, and I believed her. And for a while, it was true. Then one day, she decided she'd had enough of playing a role and returned to what she'd always been."

As infuriating as this revelation was, it was also a relief. Finally, they were getting to the bottom of his inability to see her as a hardworking woman with a mind of her own and dreams to build.

"So I'm being judged by what some other woman did?" Chloe couldn't believe this. She hadn't been working to convince him she could do the job. She'd been in competition with a memory—a bad one. And the ghost had won. "Because she was a bitch, all women are the same?"

"Not all women."

"Just the rich ones," she said.

"Basically."

"Right." Shaking her head at the stupidity of this conversation, when she spoke, her voice carried the heat of her rising temper. "You know, my great-grandfather was a wildcatter. He sunk holes over half of East Texas looking for oil. Meantime, he worked the oil fields, moving from one to the next, taking his family with him. They lived in tents, fished for their dinner and worked hard."

She was tired of being held up as somehow unworthy of respect because her family had money. Well, they hadn't always. "He and my great-grandmother had five kids, and still managed to save enough money to buy a piece of land outside Beaumont. Grandpa had a *hunch*, he always said." Liam was listening, at least. "They worked that plot of land for a solid year before they struck oil."

He took a gulp of coffee and nodded. "It's a good

story. And your great-grandfather sounds like a hell of a man. But what's your point?"

"You're deliberately stupid," she snapped, "if you don't see it. They were a team. My great-grandmother was the one holding the family together while her husband worked for their future. Their sons grew the company and their children expanded it. My point is people work for what they have, one way or another. They all do. I do."

"Yeah, but if things don't work out for you, there's always Daddy's money to fall back on, right? So it cushions the failure."

Chloe threw both hands up. "You're impossible. Okay. Answer this. If you do manage to someday find a woman who meets your impeccable standards, what happens if you have kids?"

"What?"

"Well," she said hotly, "they'll be born into money. Won't that automatically make them losers not to be trusted?"

"No," he countered, "because they won't be spoiled. Like your sister."

"Leave her out of this."

"Happily."

Wow. A fantastic night and a beautiful morning had all gone to hell in an instant. Chloe took a breath and blew it out. She wasn't going to win this. His features were blank, his eyes shuttered and he might as well have been in another county. A part of Liam had already said goodbye to her. Maybe he'd been saying goodbye since the day they met—she just hadn't heard him.

"I think I'm done with this ranching experiment," Chloe said, keeping her gaze squarely on his. "So tell me now. Pass or fail? Do I get that land you promised me? Do I stay here at Sterling's or are you going to tell him that the cowgirl camp won't work?"

"You still get the land at my place. I keep my word."

She tipped her head to one side to stare up at him. "And you won't one day decide you want something else? Change your mind?"

"No," he said, obviously insulted she'd think it.

"See," Chloe told him sadly, "neither would I. The difference between us is, I believe you. I'm willing to take the chance that you won't suddenly turn on a dime."

"Chloe—"

"Just stop," she said, both hands up. "I'm going to go pack. I'll be gone by this afternoon."

"Fine." He stood like a statue, unmoving. Unyielding. Morning sunlight drifted through the kitchen window and threw his features into a blend of light and shadow.

She'd always remember him like this, Chloe thought, as if he was caught between the past and the future. Darkness and light.

"You know, I hope you really loved her," Chloe

said, watching him. "The woman who taught you to never trust a living soul again. I hope you loved her and that losing her crushed you."

He nodded. "It did, thanks."

"Good, because now you're doing the same thing to me, and I want to make sure you know how I feel."

"What are you saying?"

"Exactly what you don't want to hear," Chloe said, lifting her chin. "I love you, Liam."

"Damn it—"

She choked out a sound that was halfway between a laugh and a cry. "Nice response. I'll treasure it always."

He took a step forward, so she backed up. If he touched her now, she just might shatter.

"It wasn't supposed to happen."

God, he was so stupid. Were all men this ridiculous, or had she just been lucky enough to fall for someone "special"?

"Well," she said tightly, "don't worry. I'm just a rich girl. I'll probably change my mind soon and won't think about you at all."

Then she left. While she still could.

Ten

A couple days later, Liam told himself this was better. With Chloe gone, there were no distractions. He could finish off his time at the Perry Ranch in some semblance of peace. Sort of. But even he didn't believe his lies.

She wasn't there physically, but she was still everywhere he looked. Their conversation in the kitchen kept repeating over and over in his mind as if it were on a loop. He could see her eyes, hear her voice, and he remembered how hard it had been to just stand there and not touch her. If he had though, it wouldn't have helped. He'd have only prolonged the inevitable.

She was different from any other woman he'd ever known, and still Liam couldn't bring himself to trust it. Trust her. He had chased what he wanted once before, and it had all gone to hell. How could he believe?

She loved him.

"Well, hell," he muttered, "I didn't ask for that. Neither of us did."

What was he supposed to do with that? Her feelings. The feelings he had and was busy denying. Liam didn't know. Didn't have any answers at all. And that bothered him because he always knew what he was doing and where he was going. Until now.

Liam stretched the string of barbed wire to the fence post and hammered it into place. He kept trying to concentrate on his work. It was his last day at the Perry Ranch after all. But his mind kept drifting and his heart ached. And that was a distraction.

But tomorrow, he'd be on his own spread. What he'd worked for. What he had the damn right to enjoy. For years he'd given his life to others. He'd protected the Perry Ranch and had helped it grow. Now it was his turn to focus on what mattered to *him*. And he couldn't let Chloe matter. Couldn't admit it even to himself. She couldn't be a part of what came next despite how good it felt to have her with him. Beside him.

His hammer hit his thumb, and that pain was

enough to take his mind off the ache in his heart. He shook his hand, hard. "Damn it!"

"Problem, boss?"

Scowling, he looked at Tim. "No. No problem." Nothing he could do anything about, anyway. "And as of tomorrow, I'm not the boss. Mike is. Remember?"

Tim grinned and went back to repairing the fence line. "That's tomorrow, boss."

Right. Typical cowhand, Liam thought. No plans beyond the day they were living. Just do the job and let the future take care of itself. Well, Liam wasn't like that. Never had been.

Now, his future was within reach. Everything he'd ever worked for was laid out in front of him—and the shining potential of it all didn't look as perfect as it once had.

Chloe's business was up and running again, but so many others weren't. For two days, she volunteered with her neighbors, sweeping out mud, carting away trash and, in general, helping out with everyone.

"Still, could've been worse," Hank Cable said. "I was living in Galveston back in '69, and what that hurricane left behind makes all of this mess look like a day in Disneyland."

Hank's hair salon was right down the street from Chloe's office, and she was not only a friend, but a customer of Hank's daughter, Cheryl. The beauticians had all turned out to help with the cleanup, but it was the camaraderie of being together that was really helping.

"Oh, Pop, you're always talking about living through Camille," Cheryl teased.

"Was a hell of a storm," he insisted. "Worth talking about. And we didn't even get the full force of the damn thing."

Chloe gathered up another trash bag and tied it closed. Everyone on the street was stacking their garbage on the curb to be ready when the city trucks were out again.

"Has the water completely receded now?" Chloe asked.

"From what I heard," a woman across the room answered, "most of the city's good now, but the low-lying areas are still pumping out floodwaters."

"Not just there," Cheryl said, "a lot of these older buildings have basements, and they were really flooded. People are scrambling to find sump pumps to clear the water out."

Taking out the trash, Chloe paused on the curb to look up and down the familiar street. Most of the damage was cleared away, though several offices still had plywood tacked up where windows used to be. A few of the trees were in desperate need of trimming because of broken branches, but that apparently was low on the priority list.

Naturally though, her gaze swung to the Texas Cattleman's Club building across from her own business. Was it really only about three weeks ago that she and Liam were forced to take refuge there? It felt like a blink of time and also as if she'd known him forever.

A work crew was setting up ladders outside the building, and she knew there were others working on the inside. She knew exactly how flooded that first floor had been and now, thanks to Cheryl, she was wondering about the old building's basement. It had to be completely underwater.

Her gaze lifted to the third floor and the bedroom where she and Liam had started the craziness. God. She missed him. She always would. But, since meeting him, she'd also learned a lot about herself. She'd worked a ranch. She'd done the job. She'd earned the respect of the other ranch hands, and more, the dreams she'd had as a child were now her reality.

She was going to concentrate on the camp. On showing the girls what it felt like to prove yourself *to* yourself. She'd build a little bunkhouse, complete with bathrooms and showers, on the land Liam had promised her. She'd be there full-time, and if that meant she had to see Liam and not have him, well, she'd have to find a way to deal with that.

Loving Liam had given her back her dreams. She didn't regret a moment of it.

* * *

The following morning, Liam's truck was packed with the last remaining things he hadn't already taken to his own place. He was ready to leave and yet, looking around the Perry Ranch, he had to take a minute. He'd lived most of his life on this spread. He'd grown up here, learned here and, thanks to Chloe, he'd loved here.

Yes. Sometime during the night, Liam had had to admit the stone-cold truth. He loved Chloe. But did that change anything? Did it mean that he could suddenly trust in something that had burned him badly the first time?

But could he even compare the two situations? What he felt for Chloe was so much more than he'd had with Tessa. He hadn't been able to acknowledge it, even to himself, but what he had with Chloe was—

"Ready to leave, are you?"

Sterling Perry's voice shattered his train of thought, and Liam watched the older man stride across the ranch yard and then step up onto the porch alongside him.

"About time, don't you think?" Liam asked. "I was just standing here thinking how I've been on this ranch since I was seven years old."

Sterling laughed and nodded. "A skinnier kid I've never seen. But you had a way with horses. Even then."

Liam glanced at the older man. Sterling wore one

of his suits, with a black Stetson and shining black boots. He looked like the Hollywood ideal of a Texas patriarch. And Liam was pretty sure Sterling knew it and played the part.

"You getting sentimental on me, Sterling?"

"That would be something, wouldn't it?" He leaned one shoulder against a porch post and shook his head. "No, I'm not. But as you get older, you do a lot more looking back than forward, Liam. And standing here today, I see you as a boy, a teenager, a young man with a head full of ideas for change."

"Yeah." Sheepishly, Liam took his own hat off and pushed one hand through his hair. "I did give you a hard time now and then, didn't I?"

"More your daddy than me," Sterling mused, staring off across the yard as if looking into a past only he could see.

"Your daddy was a good man," he said softly. "But when he lost your mother, he lost a part of himself. That softer part where love lives in a man."

Liam frowned, remembering. His mother had died not long after his father had taken the job as foreman here. A car accident on the way into Houston for some Saturday shopping. A disaster that had changed everything for Liam and his father.

Sterling turned his head to look at Liam. "It was a hard time. For both of you."

"Yeah, it was." Some men, Liam knew, would

have lost themselves in their own pain, ignoring their children, or worse yet, even running from the hard injustice of loss. Liam's father hadn't. He'd just gone on. A little harder, a little colder, but he'd been there, day in and day out.

"Losing your mother about ripped your daddy's heart out, Liam, but he didn't quit. Not once."

"No, sir." Liam took a deep breath to withstand the rising tide of old memories, and wondered where the hell Sterling was going with this.

Musing almost to himself, Sterling went on. "Takes a strong man to risk pain and keep going."

Suspicious now about the track this little conversation was taking, Liam looked at him.

Sterling met his gaze. "You've always had your plans and dreams, Liam. Being your own man, calling your own shots." He nodded sagely. "I can understand that. Respect it. But does that really mean you have to be alone?"

Liam started to answer, but the older man cut him off. "I had my Tamara, you know. We had ups and downs like anybody else. But it was a good marriage. People used to say I married her for this ranch, but the truth is, I loved that woman until the day she died—no matter what gossips have to say about things."

He hadn't paid any attention to gossip until the

night Chloe'd told him the story. Now he said what he'd told her then. "I don't listen to gossip."

"Then you're a better man than most around here." Sterling gave him a sad smile. "My point is, while you're out there building your life, and starting in on all those grand plans, you might want to pause and think about something."

Liam leaned against another porch post and listened. Sterling had been good to him his whole life. Even when he was furious with him, Liam never forgot how much he owed the man. The least he could do on his last day here was let him say his piece. "I'm listening."

Sterling grinned. "You don't want to, but you will," he said. "That hard head of yours. Blessing and a curse. You're a lot like your father, you know. He learned early this lesson I'm about to share with you.

"Plans and schemes and money and success don't mean dick, son, if you're alone." Sterling stared into the distance again and kept talking. "You find a woman who fills all the holes in your soul, then you be smart enough to grab hold of her and never let go." He paused to turn his head and stare into Liam's eyes. "Because once you've lost her, a part of yourself is gone and it won't ever come back."

A long moment of silence ticked past. Liam didn't know what the hell to say to that because every word had rung true for him. He had been walking around with a soul like a sieve, and he hadn't even noticed until Chloe started filling in those gaps.

And now that she was gone, it was as if he'd sprung a damn leak and the goodness and light inside him was draining out.

"Just something for you to think about," Sterling said, then stepped closer and clapped one hand onto Liam's shoulder. "I know you'll make that ranch of yours a big success, boy. You come around and see me sometimes, though. All right?"

He started down the steps and only stopped when Liam called his name. "What is it?"

Liam's brain was racing. He scrubbed one hand across his jaw, looked out at the stables, then back to Sterling. "The new foal. Will you sell him to me?"

Sterling looked at him for a long second or two, then a smile curved his mouth. "You take him with you. Call him a ranch-warming present." He started walking, then stopped again and looked back over his shoulder. "You can pay me for his mother though, because you'll need her, too. At least until he's weaned."

Liam grinned, then asked with affection, "You're still a cagey old bastard, aren't you?"

Sterling winked at him. "And don't you forget it."

The street outside Chloe's office was busy. Regular traffic was closed off since the recovery and cleanup efforts were still in effect. Chloe sat at her new desk, on her new computer, and went over the final details for the Farrels' anniversary party she had scheduled for the following week. Everything was in place, so there was really nothing for her to check, but she kept at it, because this was going to be not only her next job, but her *last* one.

She'd already arranged for another event planner to take over for her with the two other small parties she'd agreed to do. As soon as she'd given the Farrels the best anniversary party ever, she was going to devote herself to her cowgirl camp.

Whether Liam liked it or not, she was going to be at his ranch every damn day until she got the camp up and running. And then she'd be there every day running it.

"So he's just going to have to get used to ignoring me." She laughed to herself, as she opened her email. "He'll be great at it, probably. I'm the one who's going to have trouble with this."

She answered an email from the band she'd booked for the party, assuring them of the time and place. Then she tucked it into a Save folder and moved onto the next one.

"You could have the camp at Sterling's," she told herself. "That's still an option." But it really wasn't. "No, the spot at Liam's is perfect. The oaks, the stables. I'll just have to deal. After a while, it won't be hard to see him. Just…sad."

"What's sad?"

She jolted, and looked up to see Liam standing in her doorway. Nope. She'd never get used to seeing him. Never get over the instant flash of heat and love that filled her with one glance. And that was way beyond sad.

"You really enjoy sneaking up on me, don't you?"

He gave her a half smile and everything in her melted. Honestly, this was not fair, to have her body react to him like this even when her mind was screaming at her that there was no point.

"I guess I do."

"Wow. Honesty." Chloe closed her laptop and stood up, deliberately keeping her desk between them. "Why are you here, Liam?"

"Your place looks nice," he said, clearly stalling as he looked around the redone office.

"You didn't come here to talk about the building," she said flatly. "So why *did* you come?"

"You want honesty there, too?"

"That'd be nice, yes." God, why didn't her black slacks come with pockets? What was she supposed to do with her hands? She crossed her arms over her chest and realized she probably looked defensive. Well, good. She was feeling defensive.

"Okay." He walked farther into the room, letting the door close behind him.

He looked good. No surprise there. Black jeans,

white long-sleeved shirt with the sleeves rolled back to the elbows. He pulled his Stetson off and held it in one hand while he looked at her.

"Here's honesty for you." He took a breath, held her gaze and said, "I love you, Chloe."

"What?" She shook her head to clear it, because she couldn't believe what she was hearing. That, she hadn't been expecting. Dreaming about, hoping for, sure. But she'd thought what they had was over, so this complete 180 had her spinning in place. Still she couldn't really accept this so she said, "Say it again."

"I love you, Chloe."

Tears filled her eyes but she blinked them back. This moment was too important for blurred vision. Her heartbeat raced, pounding so hard in her chest it was a wonder he couldn't hear it.

"I'm not done." He took a step closer, tossed his hat onto her desk and said, "I do love you. But I want you to know that I also trust you, Chloe. I respect you. I know who you are and I believe it. I believe in you."

She pulled in a deep breath, hoping to steady herself, but it wasn't working. Nothing could have. He was giving her everything. She almost pinched herself to make sure she wasn't dreaming. "What happened, Liam? What made you…"

"You left," he said. "Simple as that. I thought I could handle it, that it would be better for both of us. But then, I realized that when you left you took so many pieces of me with you, I couldn't breathe."

Her heart was galloping and her blood was rushing through her veins. She fought for breath and watched his lake-blue eyes, and she saw the truth of what he was saying written there. He meant every word, and that was better than any dream she'd been chasing her whole life.

Liam smiled. "Just this morning, Sterling told me that if I found a woman who could make me complete, I should never let her go."

"Sterling Perry?" she said on a laugh of surprise.

"Yeah, shocked me, too." He came around the corner of the desk, but stopped just short of touching her. His gaze moved over her face, then back up to her eyes. "He was right. I don't want to go through my life wondering what might have happened if I'd taken the chance. If I'd trusted my gut."

"Your gut?" she repeated.

"Yeah." Liam finally touched her, lifting one hand to her cheek, and Chloe closed her eyes briefly to let that tender caress seep into her bones.

"From that first day with you, Chloe, I knew you were different than any woman I've ever known." He sighed and shook his head. "I didn't want to believe it because then I'd have to risk everything again."

He dropped both hands onto her shoulders and pulled her in closer. "But the bigger risk is living without you. Don't think I could do it. And I know I don't want to try." He slid his hands up from her shoulders to cup her face and tilt it up to him. "So instead, I'm here, apologizing for being a damn fool—"

"You actually haven't apologized yet," she interrupted, because she was feeling so happy, so relieved, she wanted to laugh.

Wryly, he said, "Well, I don't do it often, so I'm not very good at it."

Chloe actually did laugh then and felt good for the first time in days. "We'll come back to it then."

"Woman," Liam said impatiently, "if you'd just let me get this done with…"

"Right." She nodded, smiling. "Go ahead."

"I want you to marry me, Chloe. Today. Tomorrow. I can wait a week, but not much longer."

Stunned, she stared at him. "Marry you?"

He looked insulted. "Well, what the hell else am I here for?"

Chloe laughed again. This was so Liam. Irritated, impatient and completely perfect for her. "Well, if you came to propose, did you bring a ring?"

"Of course I brought a ring," he said and dug into his jeans pocket. "I didn't go shopping or anything yet, so I'll take you to the best jewelry store in Houston and you can pick whatever you want."

He held out a gold ring with three small diamonds set in a heart pattern. "This was my mom's," he said softly. "I brought it with me to seal the deal—if you said yes. But like I said, we can go shopping and you can pick out something you like."

Chloe lifted her right hand to her mouth and looked from the simple, elegant ring to the man offering it to her. The man who couldn't trust was offering her his mother's ring. He had faith in her to be with him. Stay with him. And he was proving it by offering her something that was very important to him.

"You couldn't have done anything more meaningful to me," she said.

"Yeah?" Both eyebrows went up and one corner of his mouth quirked. "So is that a yes?"

She held out her left hand and he slid the ring onto her finger. "Of course it's a yes, Liam. For you it'll always be yes."

"Thank God," he whispered and pulled her in to kiss her.

She felt everything shattered inside her come together, and all those ragged edges smoothed over as if they'd never been there at all. When she pulled back, she looked up at him and said, "I don't want another ring. I want this one."

His eyes flashed, with heat and love, warming her through. "Deal. I'll make sure the wedding band is splashy, though. How's that?"

"Just not as splashy as Ellen's," she said, laughing.

His smile faded, he looked deeply into her eyes and said softly, "You're nothing like Ellen. Nothing like anyone else I've ever met."

Now her heart was melting right along with her body. He *saw* her. He saw who she was, who she'd made herself and who she wanted to be. And he loved her. There was no greater gift.

"I love you, Liam," she whispered, and felt a sweet rush of warmth that settled around her heart and glowed so brightly she was almost surprised that light wasn't spilling from her fingertips.

"I'm never going to get tired of hearing that," he warned.

"Boy, I hope not." Chloe went up on her toes and wrapped her arms around his neck.

She couldn't believe how quickly life could turn around. How she could go from bereft to happy in a blink of time. Suddenly, she felt that anything was possible. *Everything* was possible.

He held her close, buried his face in the curve of her neck and whispered, "God, you smell good." His arms tightened around her. "I missed you, Chloe. I couldn't even be at the new ranch without you." Lifting his head, he looked down at her. "Today was moving day. Couldn't do it without you."

"You're not going to make me cry," she said with a choked laugh.

"Wanna bet?" He kissed her, then looked into her

eyes and said, "Here's your wedding present. Shadow and his mother are yours."

"What?" This she couldn't believe. That he would do this for her. That he would know just how much it meant to her. She'd been there for Shadow's birth, and leaving him had been harder than she'd wanted to admit. The tears she had refused to cry spilled over and rained down her cheeks. "Really?"

"Really. I didn't tell you that first because I didn't want you marrying me just to get that horse of yours."

She laughed, delighted with him and with the life they would be building together.

"The horses should be at the ranch by now. Tim was going to load them up and bring them to their new home." He kissed her again, then looked into her eyes. "I'm here to do the same with *you*."

"Yes, Liam. Oh, yes, Liam." She laid her head on his chest and whispered, "Let's go home."

He grabbed up his hat and her computer. She got her purse, and they headed out to his truck. The sun was out, the dirty, still under repair streets suddenly looked beautiful and Chloe could have danced all the way to the ranch.

"Hey, Liam!"

They stopped at the shout and saw one of the construction guys at the Texas Cattleman's Club waving them over. As they walked across the street, Liam kept one arm around Chloe's shoulders as if half-afraid she'd get away from him. That so worked for her.

"Hey, Bill, how's it going?"

"It's a damn mess is what it is," the man said, then nodded at Chloe. "Sorry, ma'am."

Bill was burly, with a scruffy red beard, stained white overalls, and wiry red hair sticking out from under his painter's cap. "This the lady you got stranded with here?"

"Yeah." Liam dropped a kiss on top of her head. "This is my fiancée, Chloe Hemsworth."

"Ma'am."

"We tried not to wreck anything while we were upstairs," Chloe said.

"Oh no, ma'am, it wasn't the two of you." Bill shook his head and threw a scowl over his shoulder at the open front door of the building. "This used to be a hotel sort of, you know?"

Liam nodded.

Chloe looked past Bill into the interior of the TCC and noticed a crowd gathering.

"Well, the basement of this place has been under water since the flood," Bill complained. "We finally got a big enough sump pump out here, but it's hard going getting the water out. We've got to drain it into the street, but not so fast that it'll get the storm drains blocked again."

"Sounds bad," Liam agreed.

"And the smell down there?" Bill shook his head again. "Had to come up here for some fresh air."

Inside the building, more men were gathering in a circle and Chloe tried to see what was going on. She tugged on Liam's hand. "Something's happening in there."

"What?" Bill turned around. "Guess we'd better go see."

Liam shrugged and murmured, "Yeah, I should check. Let Sterling know if something's wrong."

Just then, someone shouted, "Holy God, that's a dead body!"

Bill scurried inside and Liam was right behind him. Chloe held on to him, and they stepped carefully across tarps and supplies strewn across the damaged floor. The whole place smelled of paint and lacquer and sawdust.

"Maybe you should wait—" Liam broke off at Chloe's narrow-eyed stare. "Never mind."

Chloe was with him when the crowd of men parted, allowing them to see what they'd found. At the bottom of the stairs, floating in the muddy water, was a badly decomposed body. Chloe closed her eyes instantly and turned away. But the damage was done. She'd never forget.

"You'd better call the police, Bill," Liam said, and steered Chloe to the other side of the room.

"Was it here since the storm?" she whispered. "Were we here in the building with a dead person?"

"Looks that way." Liam's mouth flattened into a grim line. "I've got to call Sterling about this, Chloe. He'll want to know."

Sterling Perry was feeling satisfied. He'd done his good deed for the year in talking to Liam. "Hopefully, he won't mess things up with the Hemsworth girl," he murmured with a laugh. Hell, everyone on the ranch had seen Liam taking that long slide into love. It was only Liam himself who'd been blind to it.

Shaking his head, Sterling got down to business. Sunlight poured in through the office windows, and he glanced out, admiring as always, his view of the ranch he loved. Things were going well.

His construction company was back on track at the TCC building. Work on the place had been slow because half of Houston needed the equipment required to clear the place of floodwaters. Soon though, they'd have that storm behind them and they'd be ready to open up the Houston branch of the club.

Sterling intended to be the first president. Blast Ryder Currin to hell if he thought he was going to step in and take over.

When the phone rang, Sterling snatched up the receiver and said, "Perry."

"Sterling, it's me." Liam Morrow's voice sounded low, worried.

"If this is about that girl of yours," Sterling said, "I'm busy right now and—"

"It's not about Chloe."

In the background, Sterling heard voices, some muffled shouting. His eyebrows drew together. "What's going on?"

"I'm with Chloe now. We're at the TCC and something's happened."

Well hell. That didn't sound good. "What exactly's going on, Liam?"

"There's a body," Liam said. "A dead guy. In the basement."

"What?" His still sharp mind went momentarily blank.

"Yeah, listen, Sterling," Liam continued. "Apparently, he'd been there this whole time. Maybe since before the storm. The crew's been pumping out the water, and that's when they found him."

Sterling stood up slowly, his mind back in gear and currently racing. "Well, who the hell is he?"

"Don't know. We closed up the room and Bill Baker called the police."

"Damn it!" In his mind, Sterling could see the headlines already. Dead Man Found at New Texas Cattleman's Club. Murder?

This was a disaster waiting to happen. Sterling

did some fast thinking. He had to contain this some-how. Keep it quiet at least until they had an ID on the victim and a cause of death. If this got out now and the media made it a salacious story—which they happily would—it could kill the new club charter.

"All right, Liam, listen," Sterling said, rushed now, "you tell my construction crew to keep their damn mouths shut about what they found."

"All right," Liam said, "but that's not going to change anything, Sterling. The police are still on the way."

"I'll handle the police," Sterling told him. "You let the crew know that it'll mean their jobs if I hear about any of them talking to the press. Or anyone else for that matter."

Was the man dead before the storm or during it? Before, he'd have needed a key to get in. During, with the windows blown in, he could have walked in with no problem. But Liam and Chloe had been right upstairs. Too many questions, not enough answers.

Still frowning, he ordered, "We don't know any-thing so there's no point speculating with the media."

"Fine. I'll tell them. But, Sterling, like I said, the police are coming. Hell, I can hear the sirens now. You can't keep this quiet."

"Watch me." Sterling heard the sirens through the phone and rubbed the back of his neck. "Liam, when the police arrive, get the one in charge to call me once he's examined the scene. I'm going to pull in some favors with the chief and the mayor."

"Seriously, Sterling? A man's dead."

He scowled at the phone. Liam was a good man, but he couldn't see as far as Sterling could. And Sterling wasn't about to watch his plans disintegrate because some damn fool got himself killed.

"And he won't get any deader if we do this my way. Now you take care of this, Liam. We need to keep this quiet, you understand?" Sterling was gritting his teeth so hard his jaw ached. "With all the damage and injuries from this storm still being reported on, we should be able to bury this news at least for a few days. With a little time, we can spin this story the right way. I need this quiet, Liam. Handle it."

Angela Perry rushed into her father's office just in time to hear the end of the phone conversation. She'd gone to see her father, to ask him for the truth about Ryder Currin. The rumors she had heard about Ryder simply didn't add up to the man she'd spent time with during the storm.

But now, the need for that truth suddenly took a back seat. "Dad? What do you need to spin? What's happened? What are you trying to hide?"

Sterling slammed the phone receiver down, looked at his daughter and demanded, "Angela, what are you doing here?"

"This is still my home," she snapped, and thought he looked worried. Her father was never worried. Or if he was, no one could tell. He had a stone face when he needed one, which was most of the time.

"What's happened? What's going on?" She walked across the room and stopped at the edge of his desk. "Talk to me, Dad."

Grumbling under his breath, he blurted, "The construction crew found a dead body at the TCC."

"What?" Appalled, Angela could only stare at her father. "Someone's dead? Who?"

"We don't know," he admitted, clearly disgusted. "Apparently, they found the body in the basement when the crew finally started pumping the storm water out. Damn it. This is going to be a huge mess."

"A *mess*?" she repeated, stunned at her father's reaction to this news. "Someone's dead, Dad."

And her mind asked, *Who? Why? And what had he been doing at the TCC?*

Sterling shot her a hot look, but Angela wasn't cowed. She'd grown up seeing her father's temper, and she knew it was more bluster than substance.

"I don't even know what he was doing there. Maybe he took shelter at the club like Liam and Chloe did. Maybe he broke in trying to loot the place. Maybe he fell down the basement stairs and broke his fool neck." Sterling shoved both hands in his pants pockets and idly jingled the change there. "This is a disaster. If word of this gets out, it could stall the plans for the club indefinitely."

"Really?" she demanded. "*That's* what you're worried about? The club? Someone's *dead*, Dad."

"Now you sound like Liam." He frowned again. "The man's already dead. Nothing I say now will change it. All I can do is contain the situation. Stop being so soft, Angela. That's your main problem, you know. You *feel* too much and don't think objectively enough. No one gets ahead in this life by being softhearted."

Growing up, she'd heard that piece of advice more than once. "Better that than cold."

"Not cold," he corrected. "Pragmatic. There's a difference."

"Is there?"

He shook his head and when the phone rang, he grabbed it, waving at her to get her to leave.

"Detective Hansen," Sterling was saying as she left the office. "I hear we have a problem at my company's job site…"

Angela walked out of the office, and closed the door behind her. She hadn't gotten any answers about Ryder. And now, she had many more questions about this dead body.

Who was it?

What had he been doing there?

* * *

I waited for days now and no one talked about the body at the club. Just a quick mention on the news and then...nothing. Why?

I rubbed my gritty eyes and found no relief. I was so tired. Fear was exhausting.

I was constantly waiting for an ax to fall. For the other shoe to drop. For someone, somewhere to suddenly remember having seen me at the TCC. Then what? No wonder I couldn't sleep. I bet Sterling slept like a baby, the old bastard.

Had he used his influence to shut everything down? Were reporters not interested in actually doing their jobs anymore? As long as no one was talking about the murder, Sterling was safe. If word got out about the body, it would have to stall the TCC's plans for the building, if nothing else. But more, it would ruin Sterling Perry, because it was his construction company that'd discovered the dead man. The police would investigate him, looking for a connection. People would wonder if Sterling was trying to hush up a crime. People would talk. I had to do something. Get people interested. Talking. I couldn't take much more of this waiting. I had to find a way to pin this body on Sterling himself.

And yet I had doubts.

Trying to ruin the man was one thing, but framing him for murder was another. Though even if he were arrested, he'd never be convicted. How could he be? He didn't do it.

No, his reputation would be shot and his supposed good name ruined but he wouldn't go to jail.

Killing that man had been an accident. But it seemed that something good could still come of it.

I dialed the number for the Houston paper on the burner phone. I was put on Hold. I waited, waited. Finally, a reporter came on the line.

I didn't give my name. I just talked. Asked the right questions.

"Isn't it weird that a dead body was found in the new TCC building in downtown Houston? Perry Construction found the dead man, but no one's talking about it." I paused for effect. "I wonder why it's being kept so quiet... What does Sterling Perry and the Texas Cattleman's Club have to hide?"

I hung up.

Smiled.

Let's see how Sterling handled this twist.

* * * * *

Will Sterling be framed for murder?
Find out in the next installment of
Texas Cattleman's Club: Houston

Read every scintillating episode!

Hot Texas Nights *by* USA TODAY
bestselling author Janice Maynard

Wild Ride Rancher *by* USA TODAY
bestselling author Maureen Child

That Night in Texas *by Joss Wood*

Rancher in Her Bed *by* USA TODAY
bestselling author Joanne Rock

Married in Name Only *by* USA TODAY
bestselling author Jules Bennett

Off Limits Lovers *by Reese Ryan*

Texas-Sized Scandal *by* USA TODAY
bestselling author Katherine Garbera

Tangled with a Texan *by* USA TODAY
bestselling author Yvonne Lindsay

Hot Holiday Rancher *by* USA TODAY
bestselling author Catherine Mann

"You live in a secluded paradise." Rain started, a light
sprinkling that grew stronger in seconds until it lashed the
car windows. The interior immediately fogged—probably
from her accelerated breathing.

Jack smiled. "There are other houses." The wipers added
a rhythmic thrum to the sound of the rainfall. "The mature
trees make it seem more remote than it is." Rather than take
the driveway to the front of the house, he pulled around
back to a carport. "The garage is filled with tools, so Brodie
helped me put up a shelter as a temporary place to park."

Ronnie was too busy removing her seat belt and looking
at the incredible surroundings to pay much attention to
where he parked—until he turned off the engine. Then the
intoxicating feel of his attention enveloped her.

Her gaze shot to his. *Think of your future*, she told herself.
Think of how he'll screw up the job if he sticks around.

He'd half turned to face her, one forearm draped over the
wheel. After his gaze traced every feature of her face with
almost tactile concentration, he murmured, "We'll wait here
just a minute to see if the storm blows over."

Here, in this small space? With only a console, their
warm breath and hunger between them?

Did the man think she was made of stone?

She swallowed heavily, already tempted beyond measure.
A boom of thunder resonated in her chest, and she barely

noticed, not with her gaze locked on his and the tension ramping up with every heartbeat.

Suddenly she knew. No matter what happened with the job, regardless of how he might irk her, she'd never again experience sexual chemistry this strong and she'd be a fool not to explore it.

She'd like to think she wasn't a fool.

"Jack…" The word emerged as a barely there whisper, a question, an admission. Yearning.

As if he understood, he shifted toward her, his eyes gone darker with intent. "One kiss, Ronnie. I need that."

God, she needed it more. Anticipation sizzling, heart swelling, she met him halfway over the console.

His mouth grazed her cheek so very softly, leaving a trail of heat along her jaw, her chin. "You have incredible skin."

Skin? Who cared about her skin? "Kiss me."

"Yes, ma'am." As his lips finally met hers in a bold, firm press, his hand, so incredibly large, cupped the base of her skull and angled her for a perfect fit.

Ronnie was instantly lost.

She didn't recall reaching for him, but suddenly her fingers were buried in his hair and she somehow hung over the center console.

They were no longer poised between the seats, two mouths meeting in neutral ground. She pressed him back in his seat as she took the kiss she wanted, the kiss she needed.

Whether she opened her mouth to invite his tongue, or his tongue forged the way, she didn't know and honestly didn't care, not with the heady taste of him making her want more, more, *more*.

Don't miss Lori Foster's Slow Ride,
available soon from HQN Books!

Copyright © 2019 by Lori Foster

PHEXPLF0419

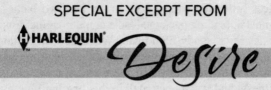
Nadia Gonzalez didn't believe in regrets. She simply did her damnedest to never make a mistake. Being careful but determined always paid off.

But there was a very good chance that Nadia had made a mistake that put her job in jeopardy. She'd done the unthinkable. She'd fallen into bed with her ridiculously hot boss. A gaffe for the ages.

But the minute she saw Matt in a perfectly tailored sleek black tux at the hospital fund-raiser last night, looking unfairly handsome, she knew she was in trouble. He almost never put on a tie. But as difficult as it was to get Matt into a suit, it turned out that Nadia had a talent for getting him out of it.

This was no small development in Nadia's life. She'd spent the past fourteen months, virtually every moment she'd been employed by Matt, secretly pining for him. He was everything Nadia could ever want in a man, the embodiment of sexy confidence, high IQ and seemingly endless brilliance wrapped up in six feet two inches of the most appealing package Nadia could imagine, topped off with thick sandy-blond hair. When he walked into a room, men and women alike turned their heads. The air crackled with electricity. His mere arrival trumpeted his greatness, and was punctuated by his bracing blue eyes. Just thinking about him made her fingers and lips tingle.

Now, driving up a steep and winding hillside to The Opulence, an hour east of Seattle, her foot gunning the gas, these thoughts of Matt were ill-timed at best.

Yes, she'd wanted Matt for a long time and they'd shared an unbelievable night of passion. But so what? Was she really willing to throw away her career? No.

Was she willing to discount the years she'd scraped by so she could make a better life for herself and her family? Absolutely not.

Matt was not the settling-down type. There would be no happy ending with him. Which meant her first priority when speaking to him today would be to make sure he understood that last night was a onetime thing. They would both be better off if they forgot about it and returned to their strictly professional dynamic.

Even though that was going to break her heart.

Will they or won't they?

Don't miss what happens next!
Tempted by Scandal *by Karen Booth*

Available May 2019 wherever
Harlequin® Desire books and ebooks are sold.

www.Harlequin.com

Want to give in to temptation with
steamy tales of irresistible desire?

Check out **Harlequin® Presents®,
Harlequin® Desire** and
Harlequin® Kimani™ Romance books!

New books available every month!

CONNECT WITH US AT:

Facebook.com/groups/HarlequinConnection

 Facebook.com/HarlequinBooks

 Twitter.com/HarlequinBooks

 Instagram.com/HarlequinBooks

 Pinterest.com/HarlequinBooks

ReaderService.com

**ROMANCE WHEN
YOU NEED IT**

PGENRE2018

Love Harlequin romance?

DISCOVER.

Be the first to find out about promotions, news and exclusive content!

Facebook.com/HarlequinBooks

Twitter.com/HarlequinBooks

Instagram.com/HarlequinBooks

Pinterest.com/HarlequinBooks

ReaderService.com

EXPLORE.

Sign up for the Harlequin e-newsletter and download a free book from any series at **TryHarlequin.com.**

CONNECT.

Join our Harlequin community to share your thoughts and connect with other romance readers!

Facebook.com/groups/HarlequinConnection

HARLEQUIN®

**ROMANCE WHEN
YOU NEED IT**

HSOCIAL2018